Kangchenjunga and Other Stories

Kangchenjunga and Other Stories

ROBERT HALSEY

PARTRIDGE
A Penguin Random House Company

To order additional copies of this book, contact
Toll Free 800 101 2657 (Singapore)
Toll Free 1 800 81 7340 (Malaysia)
orders.singapore@partridgepublishing.com

www.partridgepublishing.com/singapore

Contents

To my wife, Millicent Halsey; my son, Mark; and my daughter-in-law, Fiona, for your help and loving inspiration

Robert Halsey
2014

Kangchenzunga

Kangchenzunga is rock and ice.

Kangchenzunga dominates everything. Pandim. Kabru. Talung.

Everything.

It does not share in life and death.

It is beyond everything.

From anywhere, the massif of rock and ice can be seen on a clear day. If you look up from any street and out from any north-facing window in Darjeeling, it is there, ascendant and remote. What strength! What power! No wonder the mountain has been worshipped. In its shadow, one feels the cold, indifferent indictment of the mountain, cosmic spaces, and the chill of our littleness and insignificance. One feels a certain humility about the mountain's transcendence and magnificence. Up there broods an indifference to man's adulation and devotions; it seems to menace by its indifference.

The Darjeeling late afternoon was clean, crisp, and cold. Yesterday's maximum had barely reached ten degrees – and that only briefly before plunging sharply into negative territory before sunset. In the market, they were saying snowfall was near. We had been drinking my Glen Livet when I heard a crashing of burning logs in the grate behind me. Someone got up and stoked the grate. I stood at the window, mesmerized by the mountain, struggling with something akin to guilt and confusion.

I heard Deju say something to Dr Carr. I had met the two three weeks ago for the first time. All that I knew about Dr Carr was that he was with CARE and had been down from Gangtok many times. Deju was a local *lapcha* who claimed he too had been to Gangtok many times. A chance meeting had brought us together at the Oberoi Everest for dinner one night. Deju was an enigma. I never found out how Carr ever came to know him, and Carr never said. I've heard that his type is common enough, the type of westernized Indian who finds the company of European tourists congenial but not for baksheeh, money that is often demanded with a whine. If not wealth, his background at least suggested a certain sufficiency, as with his education. I knew nothing about him except that he was always preaching a brand of separatism, which would one day land him in trouble with the Indian security. There was a curious increase in the political unrest that was starting up in these eastern hills regions. I hoped he wouldn't get some unwary tourists trapped in open sedition. I let Deju know I wasn't interested in the political destinies of these people in any way. Nor was Carr, who shut him up no sooner than he started. It didn't deter Deju, who today was ranting on about his people, the lapchas, who had neither cultural nor political sympathies with Indians. I heard Carr rumble something inaudible in reply. The majesty of Kangchenzunga rendered void any attractions we might have had for issues of justice and self-determination. It had seen it all before.

An Ambassador taxi groaned up the steep drive, and two well-dressed Indians got out. It was clear that they weren't hills people. Over the years, hills people and Indians had come to tolerate each other in order to keep the peace. The new arrivals were given rooms adjacent to ours. They ran up the steps, stamping and blowing their hands as they went in. A door slammed, and the ambassador pulled away.

"No. No. We can't take it anymore, I tell you. We are not Indians. Look at me. Do I even look Indian?" he urged us, leaning into our faces. Dr Carr chuckled and let out a stream of pipe tobacco smoke. Through the slight haze of bluish smoke, he remonstrated lightly that you can't tell an Indian by what he looks like – nor anyone else, for that matter. Deju complained that the matter deserved more serious attention than Carr was prepared to offer. Deju's Sino features blazed with revolutionary ardor.

"You British are responsible for everything, for the mess we are in, and you don't seem to care. You lot sold us out," he said.

"Sold you out, did we?" sighed Carr.

I was keeping well out of this. I was getting quite tired of Deju by this time. Outside, two Nepalese urchins threw gravel at each other and raced away jabbering excitedly.

"Yes, sure you did. Why didn't you restore our lands to us? Why didn't you return our autonomy to us? You claimed to be applying the principle of self-determination. So Kashmir was returned to a single Hindu family although you knew it had over ninety per cent Muslim population. And over here, Nagas, Lapchas, and Mizo were handed over from one overlordship to another, and New Delhi became our capital by force. We went from one form of slavery to another. You couldn't get out of India quick enough – so … so you merely …"

Deju threw his hands up into the air and paced the floor in the finest theatrical tradition. I caught his entire act in the reflection of the windowpanes. This was the direct benefit of my Glen Livet. Outside, a heavy mist was rolling down the sides of the mountain, obscuring the village and pouring through the clusters of pines and firs obscuring shanties perched precariously at the edges of precipices. The golden dome of the Buddhist monastery blinked before it too disappeared. I inhaled deeply. The vents in the roof brought in the delicious smell of peanuts being roasted on charcoal. The vendors would still be bent over their earthen stoves, earnestly engaged in plying their business. I finished the last of my whiskey and fell into a dreamlike trance.

*****

The monkey temple … I was back in my guilt. From the moment I stepped into the ruined temple and set my eyes on her, I knew that she was desperately ill. She lay in a plastic sleeping bag with a cotton blanket thrown over her in a pathetic attempt to keep her warm. The contents of her backpack lay scattered about. A camera here, a diary there. A book nearby. I picked it up. Rilke! Her blond hair was matted with the heavy sweat of a wasting fever. Her breathing was labored. She was so small. She looked to be no more than an adolescent. I saw fear in her eyes as she saw me. She moaned. Near her lay a syringe.

*****

"Deju, I can sympathize with you. I really can. Believe me. I am not taking you lightly at all. One cannot work six years in India for CARE and not notice certain things. But look, my work is with children. I really have no politics in India. I cannot. My work takes me to Darjeeling, Gangtok, NEFA, and Dhaka. So yes, I see things. I feel things, but I have my work too." Deju shrugged, lit another cigarette, and smoked silently for a while.

"OK," he said finally. Just that and nothing more. I can't say why, but the ensuing silence made me turn around and face them. I made a great show of rubbing my hands together enthusiastically.

I said, "I've got a great idea. Why don't we get something to eat? It's nearly twelve. The food is excellent at the Oberoi Everest."

Dr Carr agreed, probably more to get away from Deju's hectoring and histrionics than from any real hunger pangs. He knocked his pipe against the grate and cleaned the bowl of his pipe. The mood had changed.

On our way there, Deju gave us some entertaining highlights of last summer at the Oberoi Everest, which never failed to attract only wealthy tourists, most of whom were Germans.

Lunch turned out to be a quiet affair. Hunger, not politics, took our attention.

They served a good biryani there. The salads were also a treat. Coffee was from a surprising Indian blend. It was thoroughly satisfying.

*****

Now that I think of it, the morning that I left, Shenju- La had been freezing. I had to blow repeatedly on my gloves to keep me warmer. I tried stamping to keep the cold from my feet. The sky had lightened gradually; dawn made a belated and reluctant entry. Suddenly, a woman's shrill scream of anger shattered the early morning silence. I looked around the clearing in the forest, trying to determine what was happening and to whom, but I couldn't discern anything. The world had returned to its eerie silence. A pink fringe slowly poured over the shoulders of the mountains, none higher and more magnificent than Kangchenzonga. It was stunningly beautiful.

The sun's rays gradually reached the lower heights, penetrated the valleys, and lit up the villages from where wood fires from cottages were already pouring out. I checked out my packs, got into my jeep, and headed off to the Sikkim border. Recollections of that day still bring up the chill I felt then. Once past the tea estates, the roads deteriorated rapidly because of ongoing neglect.

In some places on the shoulders of the mountains, there was no road, and the rear wheels of the jeep spun wildly and frighteningly in the air. The scree fell away noisily into the gorges of swiftly flowing streams and rivers. I bounced about crazily, my heart in my mouth and my lungs bursting with fear.

I eventually came to a small village, where I managed to terrify some poultry out of my way. I now knew that Shenju-La wasn't far off. If the weather wasn't bad, I usually spent a little time in the ruined temple just to rest up a bit, as I did that day. It gave me three canvases and a meditation. I liked to come here at least once a year. Anyone who has experienced Kangchenzonga just once is forever a slave to it. But that day, sadly, there was something more to it than that mountain's uncompromising grandeur.

*****

On his upper right lip, Dr Carr had a mole that I hadn't noticed before. It became a part of the ironic smile he awarded Deju's political jibes. Uninvited, Deju had made himself a regular at the table whenever we had meals. We didn't really mind, but he had taken it all for granted. At times, he had kindly insisted and settled the account, much to our delight.

"Hardstaff, I don't suppose you know any of these Germans around the place, do you?" asked Carr. This almost floored me, and I froze involuntarily.

"No. Of course not. I can't imagine whatever made you ask such a strange question, Carr," I replied, a bit aggrieved but a lot more surprised.

Carr gave one of his grunts and let it slide. I pointed out that I usually passed some fifty or sixty of them after I passed

Ghoom when I was on the approaches to Darjeeling. They came in large numbers every year. The ones he was referring to were a motley lot of backpackers, the men invariably bearded. The more affluent rode Sherpa cabs in and around the place and stayed in the better class hotels. The women were mostly blondes with wild, scruffy hair. They all smoked pot whenever they felt the need to. You could smell it on them. Somehow, Ursula George was different. I'm not quite sure in what way. I thought about her often. Now my breath had returned, and I felt relieved.

"Actually, I am sort of acquainted with one or two, but I can't say I know them," I replied shortly. "More out of curiosity than anything. There was an ornithologist out from Munich. I have a problem remembering German names. Anyway, we're all transients here. One never comes to know anyone in the short time one has. Here today and so on and so forth. Besides, how well do we know each other, for that matter?"

"Quite," responded Carr quickly. "Come on – let's get down to the foreigners' registration office this morning, seeing we both have to be leaving. These areas are under military control, remember."

We trudged down to the tent, where soldiers stood without looking particularly menacing. They cradled their rifles and looked about them.

"By the way, Carr, why the interest in German tourists?"

"Oh, well, nothing really. It's just that the police were inquiring after some young German woman who seems to have gone missing," he replied indifferently. Before setting off, he lit up his pipe and puffed lustily.

We hung about the registration office tent, waiting to be called up. A sentry looked us up and down suspiciously. I smiled at him, trying to appear friendly and disarm any fears. It didn't seem to work. Eventually, Deju spoke to him in his own language. That did the trick. The sentry looked into the tent and shouted something to someone. A heavily moustachioed Nepalese officer came out with a steaming cup of tea and stared at us. We got our turn at last. We were impressed at how successful Deju apparently had been, and we thanked him profusely.

On entering the tent, we saw a large Indian flag. It formed the background to a table with sheets of paper covering it disorderly. On one side of the table was a Petromax light and on the other a field telephone. Two officers got together and scrutinized what must have been some photographs of us, looking searchingly at us a couple of times. We were glad we passed muster eventually. Our authorization papers were in order, duly signed, and thunderously stamped before they gave them to us. By the time all security was in place, we noticed that we had begun losing light. I had to make my move now. I abruptly stopped. Carr and Deju, who had gone ahead, stopped and looked back. Carr asked what was wrong.

"I say, Winston, I wonder if you can do me a favour," I began. I hoped I didn't sound desperate or in need of assistance. I didn't want to arouse any suspicion.

"Yes. Yes, of course," he replied, clearly a bit puzzled. "Anything wrong?"

"Wrong? No. I thought I'd take a few shots of the view here and catch up a little later. And there are also a few loose ends to see to before I finally leave here. I hope you guys don't mind. We'll meet at Teesta in a day or two. How's that?" I said.

"Regular man of mystery is our Hardstaff, eh?" laughed Carr. "Yeah, sure. There's no rush. Should be OK. We could in a few days too," he added.

"No, please."

I had undoubtedly created a mystery and couldn't handle it now. Carr blinked and removed his pipe from his mouth. He and Deju looked at each other for a few moments that seemed to take an eternity.

"Please," I beseeched them firmly.

"OK, then I will go along with the good doctor," said Deju.

"Yes. That's OK with me. Yes. All right, then. Take care. We'll carry on."

Deju nodded enthusiastically.

"Whenever you are ready, we'll meet up at Teesta like you said. OK? Near the bridge. Be sure to get there before sundown. Right?

It suited me fine. I was greatly relieved that everything had gone well. I assured them I would meet them at Teesta by sundown, if not earlier. With that, we parted company. I watched them go before I felt safe to do what I felt I had to. This could be seen as an act of deception, I suppose. What worried me a bit was that I felt no real remorse. It was just something I had to do. I recalled how I first met the helpless young German woman who looked to be a little more than an adolescent. This was when I first met Ursula George. She had been running a high temperature as she lay sweating in the ruins of the temple that was overrun by creepers and plants. Up there at about eight thousand metres above sea level lay a human being, deserted, alone, and close to death, that magnificent mountain exhibiting nothing more than a granite-like indifference. Life didn't matter to the mountain. What was even worse was that it seemed her friends shared that indifference.

I must admit that despite our leave-taking, I had no intentions of meeting up with Deju and Dr Carr at Teesta. I had lied. My meeting with the German woman had created a strange "bonding", if I could call it that. I had no idea where to go with that now. I knew that Carr could not wait for me at Teesta – not for more than a day at the most. He had a CARE conference to attend. He would need to drive down to Siliguri as soon as possible to meet the other delegates attending the meeting. That left Deju, who could be relied on to attach himself to some other interesting foreigners with whom to spend time.

And so it was that I felt no guilt as my jeep bucked and groaned up the bridle path to Shenju-la and the ruins of the monkey temple. I wondered what I would find. I could not, try as I might, get that fevered face out of my mind. The mystery of her fate moved me deeply. What was a dying German, so young, doing alone on a slope of the gigantic Kangchenzonga? There could not be a simple solution. The awful agonized groaning, the fetid darkness of the ruins, and its smell.

The shoulder of Kengchenzonga fell away sharply as the jeep negotiated its final stage of the journey. Snow had fallen – the first snows of winter which as yet lay thinly over the earth in accumulations, not able to completely conceal the undergrowth.

This was the land of the Rung-nyo-ung-dut, the demon who trapped people with its invisible chains. The people died soon after that but were allowed to roam amongst the living. The living presence of the myth was manifested by the sound of its breathing and the flitting shadows and muted echoes one heard rolling in the valleys below. The natives believe that the forests were teeming with demons. Perhaps it was the distances and the vastness of Kangchenzunga that fed our fears. Most of us would find it impossible to believe all that, but scepticism has been known to wilt under the energies generated by such experiences. The huge massif of rock and ice dominated everything and everyone, including thought, which becomes nothing but a clouded perception. Against it, nothing matters. It is totally indifferent to the fate of man. Occasionally from the peak would come rumblings that ran from peak to peak like thunder. Pandim, Kabru, and Talang exchanged whispers from time to time. Here were living elements of prehistory preserved in the language of Kangchenzonga and translated into local folklore.

*****

I stopped the jeep, yanked up the handbrake, and got out. A fine drizzle like a gentle spray was gently blowing about.

It was freezing. Snow was imminent. I couldn't stay long. The bridle paths would become coated with a fine ice, always proving dangerous. I climbed over a ruined wall over which briars were sprawling. I slipped over a boulder and sent an empty can of Hahn clanging down the slope. I stiffened and looked about me, expecting the Hahn to be detected by a man, beast, or angry demon confronting this intrusion. Nothing happened. Soon after, I felt the hard-beaked Rung-nyo-ung-dutt somewhere near at hand but invisible. I believed that if I found the demon, I would find Ursula George. In the ruins, the damp smell closed in on me like a palpable presence. The cold wind that had whipped up had died down. Now and then, I heard a tuneless whistle start up and die away in the pine tops. I took out a pocket torch and turned it on. I looked around. Nothing.

I spent some time exploring the ruins, hoping to find evidence that she had been here – passport, beads, an airline ticket, diary – anything that could link me to her. It was as though she had never existed, yet I thought I caught the stench of her fever. I sat down. No, there was no imagining it. It made me shake my head. She could not have left the place by herself. I doubted that she could have lived another twenty-four hours alone. Could her friends have returned for her? I wondered. If they hadn't, then who could have removed her? I wondered if she lay dead somewhere in the forest.

I came out of the ruined temple and scouted around in a hundred-metre radius. Neither soil nor vegetation had been disturbed. High up from the storm-covered summit came a strange sort of cry: "Was wirst du tun, Gott, wenn ich sterbe?"

What, indeed, God, would you do if I died? What does God always say?

Nothing.

Or was it the Rung-nyo-ung-dutt?

Then I found her. She was all alone. Suddenly, the cave yielded her up to the world. I thought this must be a hallucination, yet it was too real. It couldn't have been. We were back in the cave. How was this? Was I dead? What was happening to me?

This was all there was. This was all there had always been. Nothing more. There was no reply. Her eyes were shut. She was burning up. She needed urgent medical attention, but there were no telephones on the rugged and forested slopes of this mountain. Communication was impossible. Her tongue kept snaking out of her parched lips. Her tiny fists were clenched.

"Rudi," she kept calling – and something else which I couldn't quite catch.

"Rudi? Wo bist du? Bitte sag mir." She wanted to know where he was.

"Rudi?" I asked, wanting some more information about who he was.

"Du bist gegangen Du bist gegangen? " she called softly, again and again.

She was close to death. Her breathing was a gurgle at times. I could almost feel the heat from her body. The interior smelt of decay. All around was darkness, within and outside. In the innermost core was a small black straining phallic core where dead flowers lay, a sad touch of irony. Here sprawled poor Ursula George. None of this made any sense. Maybe this was life. None of it made sense unless what you made of it. Language was made to make some sense of the inscrutable if the imagination was able to invent this reality.

"Was wirst, Gott, wenn ich sterbe? " she quoted from Rilke. Through the ages, God has never answered this question.

*****

I left her to the protection of the temple. A dying woman not much older than an adolescent had been abandoned here to die a horrible death in the icy winds at the base of Kandchenzonga. I took refuge in my jeep, where I tried to hide myself from the moral squalor. In a way, I was glad to slip behind the steering wheel to feel a measure of control over something within my capabilities, something I could understand and direct. I rejoiced in the surge of energy. I felt revitalized. Its shuddering start returned me to the land of the living.

The drive down to Bagdogra Airport later in the day was mercifully uneventful. After I had retrieved the special case containing my three canvasses from the jeep, I engaged a Sherpa driver to return the jeep to Sikkim, but only after we had shared a meal and a hot, steaming cup of tea. The Sherpa was an opportunist who talked in broken English all the time. I learned all about his family, who dealt in jade and furs. He could supply me with all the jade I wanted.

New furs were being smuggled out of Tibet every day. His brother was a supplier who would be happy to let me have some at a reasonable cost. I politely fended off all his offers, and we parted company the best of friends after I slipped him some extra money as a friendly gesture.

After the jeep had noisily tooted a farewell and disappeared behind a cloud of dust, I took myself down to the customs and immigration checkpoint. Once within the comparative shelter of the transit lounge and away from strong winds, aggressive coolies, and cadaverous beggars desperately demanding baksheehs to get some food, I found a seat, sat down, and closed my eyes to relax and let the stress out of my system. What I could not succeed in doing was disengaging from this reality and getting Ursula out of my mind. I began to feel responsible for her.

Later, after I felt a bit better, I scouted around, found a newsstand, and bought a paper. It was then that I became aware of two young bearded Germans. Their backpacks and bedrolls lay on the floor between their feet. What drew me to them as I watched from a short distance was the hurt of their silence. Each seemed a spiritless shell. Their eyes were fixed on the floor, as if they were searching for a secret pattern in the mosaic.

I went over to the Air India counter and handed over my luggage. The small transit lounge was now filling up and alive with passengers on the move. They were all accompanied by all the usual throngs of well-wishers seeing them off. They were getting quite noisy. My manoeuvres had brought me surreptitiously near to the forlorn couple, and I heard one ask the other,

"Rudi, hilf mir – hilf mir, bitte …" He was clearly troubled and struggled with guilt.

I lost the rest in a sudden flare-up of conversation near me. I cursed the lot under my breath. Hans whispered something gently under great strain. They picked up some belongings and moved along with the throng of pushing passengers. They picked up their luggage and began moving along to the exit as a metallic voice called for all passengers flying to New Delhi to board the aircraft. They passed close to me. I heard Rudi mumble to himself quite dramatically as if reciting something he recalled, "Was wirt du tun, Gott, ich bin bange." His heart and mind were plainly overloaded in angst as he made his confession to his secret God. Suddenly, there was a barrier of multicoloured saris between them and me as the women pushed past. The two Germans had increased the distance between us.

I quietly called out, "Hans." I wanted to know him. To find out about Ursula George. To let them know, in fact, that I knew about their secret.

The blond man, who was taller and appeared gentler, almost effeminate, turned in fear and looked about him. He looked into faces about him furtively. He looked back a couple of times and said something to the other man, who appeared to ignore him. On his face, I thought I saw fear, guilt, and what passed for suffering.

Once I felt the shuddering, trundling wheels of the airbus as it roared under me, I gave my attention to the *Times of India*. Only once did I look out the port side window. Below me, standing out in magnificent dramatic show lay the Himalayan arc, indifferent to life and death and everything human.

I got to know Rudi and Hans at Palam airport in New Delhi. I asked if I could join them at their table for coffee and something to eat. They were cautiously obliging with faint welcoming smiles one extends to strangers under such circumstances. We discussed Sikkim, the weather, and other things, but they weren't too keen to open up on trekking and reticent about Ursula George when I turned the conversation around to her. They were shocked at how much I knew about her. Hans blinked several time, visibly moved. He cautiously asked me questions in halting English about her last movements. I had hoped to get her whole story, but the state they were in made that impossible. They did say that they had promised her, if possible, that they would return with a doctor if they could find one, bringing some medical supplies. However, on the way down, they lost their way and were only just able to find their way to Bagdora, where I met up with them. By then, they were too consumed by guilt, sorrow, and spreading panic. They believed that it was too late to find her again and that it would be too difficult explaining what had happened; besides, they were too scared by then, scared of being detained, interrogated, and losing their visas. They had panicked. They had experienced something that they scarcely understood. Betrayal rarely ever is. I wonder if they had really escaped the mountain or whether it had them in thrall.

*****

It was late in the sixth day when the *bongthin* reached Mt Kangchenzunga, where the two *rotmung* had fled. Over the flint-sharp outcrop, the shaman stopped. He called loudly into the wind. His voice carried into every crevice and pinnacle, returning to him in dying eddies of sound. He sprang like a mountain goat from rock to rock as he crossed mountain streams, his white mane flying out behind him.

"Go back, go back!" called the rotmung from all around him. He heard their words above the cascades as freezing water swirled over and between rocks.

A black cloud came rolling down from the rum-lying, the land between earth and sky. The sun was blotted out, and the sacred bongthin shivered. He wrapped his yak hair cloak tighter around him. With a swift motion, he managed to snatch back his staff from invisible preying hands. He levelled it in the direction of some mountain bramble in front of him. A loud crackling sprang out from the undergrowth. Some shrubbery was blown away up the sides of the mountain and some down the side of the ravine. Cries of unendurable pain rang out in all directions.

Shrill voices called from all sides and echoed on and on in the valleys. "Find peace, shaman. Leave the mountain. You cannot have her. Such things come and go. That is as it has been and will endure. Go back!" The convergence of the mung, or evil spirits, made it difficult for the bongthin to advance any farther. He clung to his staff. As long as it was in his keeping, the mung couldn't harm him.

"Go back, go back!" called the sharply insistent rotmung. The shaman's white beard and streaming white hair whipped about him, blurring his vision from time to time. There was a movement behind the clump of rocks. It was the mountain squirrel. At last, his friends were catching up to him. He felt his strength returning. The wild boar couldn't be too far behind. The squirrel leapt on top of the largest rock, reared up on his hind legs, and called out to him, "Oh, shaman, look to tomorrow! The fiery peacock arrives with certain death for the demons who fear it more than anyone else."

Up and down the ridges, the trill of fear could be heard rising and falling in ripples as the evil spirits called to one another. Once or twice out there, somewhere in the summit through the mist, thunder rolled.

"You well know the way of life, shaman. You were there when the waters turned to rocks, when the winds were turned to flesh and bodies, and seeds were strewn in the valleys. Go back. Go back!" The boar, the squirrel, and the bongthin spent the lengthening hours together, but as the hours passed, they knew the fiery peacock had withheld its support. The winds had died down. The whispering and whistling ceased as the mung folk made their way back over the conifers, rocks, and ice to the eternal heights. Dark mists rolled up the mountain, and the light from the sun broke through. They looked about them to see where they had landed.

Below in the valley, the shaman saw the Long-thum monastery. Lamas were moving slowly about their morning devotions. The boar and the squirrel suddenly left him. He had turned to speak to them and to entreat them to stay with him, but he was now alone. He made his way down to the monastery. No one paid him any attention. He climbed the steps and entered the dim candlelit interior. He met no one inside. When he came out again, it was near the end of the day, but he no longer had his staff. Monks passed him by, talking to one another as he strode past them up the steep goat track by which he had descended.

It took him a whole month to reach Kangchenzonga, but not before the rains set in. He was lashed by the sharp, cutting rain and high winds. In a clearing were the remains of the monkey temple. This was the land of the Rung-nyo-ung-dut, who watched his every step. He stopped and looked at the ruins for a long time. He blinked mechanically from time to time. All emotions drained from his eyes. It would soon be night, time to visit the village where the first fires for the evening meal would be burning. Then he heard her briefly, her voice drifting in the swirling winds.

"Shaman, lern vom Wind und vom Eis. Was ewig ist, wird night immer verstanden. Schauf auf die Spitze von Kangchengzonga und uberzeuge dich von dem, was unwandelbar ist und night vollends begriffen warden kann. Lausche dem Wind, bongthin. Was horst du?"

Ha, learn the way of the wind and ice! He had his existence in their very midst. He should know that better than anyone. He was painfully aware of what could and could not be. The mountain had no power over him except when he gave it that power, if he ever did.

*****

I felt a surge of creative fulfilment and a quiet exaltation. I stepped back from my canvas and cleaned my brushes. I used a knife to scrape off the extra hardened lumps of colour that I had allowed to form on my palette to be part of the picture. I washed my hands and dried them. It was all over. I had always wanted to live and move in the Himalayan mountains. I had often felt the surge within me. This was my first canvas after my return from Sikkim.

I looked at the painting again. I saw Kangchenzonga, the mighty mountain. I saw the shaman again. The demons. Ursula George. Rock and ice. The rotmung looked at me with a growing urgency. I heard the winds cry around the ruins of the temple. From the ageless peak again came the distant cry of the young woman. For just a moment, it lived in the wailing of the winds. I lost the words but none of the pain. Even though time and distance had restored to me the ability to separate my reality from the other, I knew that next fall I would be preparing to fly out again, into the mountains of Sikkim, to Kangchenzonga, where neither pain nor joy exists just the sheer mastery of the mighty mountain that rises up into the clouds, up above the transient flow of human life. It is there that one stands on the threshold of two worlds.

The Search for Lama Guchin-Alwe

The mist clung to the slopes that reared precipitously to the sharp razor ridges of the Teng-tua-lan mountains of the western pocket of Lohit. Pine needles, wet and cold, carpeted the earth. In the diluted light of dawn, a cheerless but awesome world was slowly defined detail by detail. Beads of moisture dripped from overhanging branches above them.

Huddled together, their backs to the trunks of pines, twenty or so figures sat shivering and wet, eyes furtively darting from bush to bush. Their quilted coats were thinly padded with cotton. Woollen caps made out of yaks hair and wool were pulled over their ears. The less fortunate pulled ragged bits of canvas and hessian over their bony frames. Heads down, they began to sing softly and sadly.

The others sat silently, fear filling their stretched eyes. Steamy trickles drifted from nostrils, and their teeth chattered. A woman eased herself where she sat huddled in a group of three others under a coarse grey threadbare blanket that was too small for them.

They were the first to see the green-quilted figure in baggy greenish trousers come slowly up the slope. No one spoke. All eyes were on him. What looked like an ill-fitting balaclava covered his head. He came up to them and sat down cross-legged. He scooped up a fistful of damp pine needles. He seemed to know that he was expected to say something.

"Lapokas down there," he said.

This was followed by silence which seemed to send another chill into the other gypsies.

"Chin lapokas?" a man asked, getting to his feet. He wrapped his arms across his chest and shivered. "Five days we run and hide, run and hide – here they also come. Chinese soldiers shoot all."

"Chin! Chin!"

"Chinese soldiers! Chinese soldiers!"

The four women clung closer together and began moaning.

"Shh," a chorus of frightened voices hissed at them, but they moaned even louder.

One of the gypsies, a cadaverous man, came down to the quaint squatting green figure.

"Sam Dipp, what soldiers are these? Do we have to start running again?" he asked.

One of the women cried out, "No, no more for me! I cannot run anymore."

The women under the blanket began to cry out as well. They too felt that they had had enough.

"Khampas! Khampas!" said Sam Dipp repeatedly.

Not long after, the Khampas suddenly appeared. They looked fierce in their long brown coats which reached down to their ankles. The coats showed them to be Kanga tribesmen, the fiercest of all the Khampa tribes. They held all others in contempt, especially slaves and serfs of the lamaseries. They lived between far eastern Tibet and the borderland of Arunachal Pradesh, in Northeast India. They didn't let the border stop their crossings, claiming it was all their legitimate lands anyway.

Some Khampas were booted. Their round, fat faces looked about them with a fierce arrogance. They adopted a cautious approach, spears held out before them. Others were armed with long knives, whilst another four fingered the triggers of their rifles. The foremost looked as though he had been wounded. His forehead was bandaged. He held his rifle in one hand and the other on his hip, a show of arrogance. These rifles were modern and would have been captured in some previous encounter. Now confident that they wouldn't be attacked, he strolled into the middle of the camp, ferret-like eyes missing nothing.

He turned to his men and barked, "Tulus!"

A Khampa with a curved blade spat. "Dirty gypsy vermin! What are they doing here?" he asked with a curse.

"Running like everyone else," laughed the bandaged one, who was evidently their leader.

"Even these worthless thieving ones run from the Chinese. One set of thieves running from another set of thieves! Bah!"

Kang tribesmen were the fiercest of all the Khampas in eastern Nepal and adjoining parts of Tibet and Assam. They shared a contempt for all others and saw them as slaves or serfs of the lamaseries. The Khampa chief paused near the bowed green figure, and with a swoop of his hand, he snatched the warm woollen headgear off Sam Dipp's head. With a shove, he sent Sam Dipp rolling down the slope. Then he pulled the cap over his own head and stuck his chest out in a grand pose. His men laughed raucously and made several suggestions to which – to Sam Dipp's good fortune – the chief turned a deaf ear. In the growing silence, the chief bellowed at Sam Dipp.

"Where is Lama Guchin Alwe?"

There came no answer. Sam Dipp remained prone on the grassy floor in sullen silence. The women above him began to weep and cackle in a sort of high-pitched falsetto.

"Where is the Lama Guchin Alwe?" roared the Khampa chief in growing frustration. The slope of the mountain echoed like a misty oracle. The Khampa chief looked threateningly about him and then promptly swung his rifle behind his shoulder and ambled off, joining his men. Into the eddying growing waves of mist, he and his men disappeared.

The mist soon engulfed both earth and sky but let in a pale filtered sunlight. Sam Dipp jumped to his feet and made off in the direction of the Khampas.

"Where are you going?" a man called after him.

The rest of them hurriedly collected their belongings and followed them.

"Where are you going, Sam Dipp?" called another man.

"Come on! Come on! Keep close to the Khampas," Sam Dipp replied. He knew that however much the Khampas had open contempt for the Tulus, they were still the only protection they offered, however tenuous that might have been.

Now they were gaining mobility at last as they all took after their leader. The younger and more agile began leaping and running down the slopes wherever they were to be found. The women in their long brown skirts brought up the rear. No one cared about them.

Sam Dipp and the youngest had long since disappeared from view in the thickly wooded slopes that they came to. They crashed on down, through briar and nettle. Tearing and clutching at bushes, the group eventually came across Sam Dipp. He was peering over a precipice and into the depth below, where a river ran. Sam Dipp pushed his way past the others, clearly oblivious to their heaving and panting.

"Come on! Come on!" urged Sam Dipp as he ran along another tangent. His padded coat had been torn, and some white wool peered out. He heard a scream and a crashing of branches and bushes somewhere below and knew the others were not too far off. Sam Dipp and two others jumped across the river where it had narrowed. Four shots rang out, the echoes reverberating across the valley. The two nearest Sam Dipp jerked in the air crazily like puppets and hit the water with a splash. Red threads flowed out into the water from the bodies and swirled away into the rest of the river. By this time, the other Tulus appeared, and they were terrified at what they saw. They drew back in alarm. Sam Dipp had doubled up over his folded hands. He looked at the Khampa warriors who had made an appearance from the other side of the river. They held their swords and rifles, ready for an attack. The leader with the recently acquired cap ejected his shells from his rifle noisily and came down to examine the bodies in the water.

"Bah! Same Tulu fools who know no better. A waste of precious ammunition. How many shots wasted?" he asked.

The nearest Khampa, who was the marksman, answered, "Four."

The leader's face screwed up. "Four!" the leader screamed. "Damn these Tulu fools. What a waste of ammunition. Stupid sheep. Evil, foul-smelling sheep."

The other Khampas had emerged and were ringing the banks. These sported only swords, machetes, and spears. On the other side, Tulu women had fearfully reached the scene by then and were staring stonily at the two lifeless forms in the water. The water was beginning to run red. The Khampa chief and his men glared angrily at the gypsies.

The Khampa chief lashed out heatedly at the dejected cowering lot. "What madness is this! What foolishness that cost two of you their lives … Rushing into a Khampa troop like this!"

Some Tulu men and women cried out," Do not kill us as well!"

"We are your slaves!" called out a group of men.

"Bah!" The chief waved aside the cajoling servile. "You are no better than your silly women. You are more cowardly than they are. Who would want the likes of you for slaves, anyway?" From the Khampa pack came sniggering and laughter in support of their leader. One of them pulled a young woman aside and struck her with the breadth of the sword on her posterior. Squealing, she darted behind the nearest bush. This sent the other women scattering in her direction. The Khampas might have followed them had Sam Dipp not come to the fore to create a diversion.

"Great and Khampa god-king of war, let me be of service to you. I know what you want. Let me guide you to Lama Guchin Alwe," he whispered. He came forward cringing, fully expecting the worst.

"What!" shouted the Khampa chief in anger. "You knew and kept quiet all this time. You dog! Why haven't you spoken out long before this, you … you …" He didn't continue, clearly at a loss for words at the stupidity of it all. When Sam Dipp hadn't spoken for a fairly long time, the chief strode up to him and stared into his face. He stepped aside and felled Sam Dipp with a single blow.

"Hei-fu!" he shouted to the nearest warrior, who stood nearby with a rifle at the ready. The Khampas had spread out, flanking the gypsy mob. They weren't taking any chances.

"Get this miserable dog to tell you all he knows. And you don't have to be gentle with him."

Hei-fu went down and sat by the rueful Sam Dipp. He took him by the hair, shook his head, and questioned him rapidly. He shook every word out of the fallen Sam Dipp. The Khampa chief stood looking on at the interrogation. As Hei-fu came up to report, he spat something he had in his mouth.

"The clumsy dialect of these wanderers is terrible to listen to. I can't quite make out what the idiot is babbling. It appears that the Holy Lama of Shian-fu has been taken to a safer place, where the god-king went. These tried to follow the train to Tezpur but got lost." The bloodied chief nodded his head a few times. Silence settled for a while as he decided what the next best move was. While he went over and consulted with one or two others, a Tulu crept down to the river and released a scarf belonging to one of the dead Tulus. It had been caught between a rock and a ridge. He retrieved the blood-soaked article and rinsed it out. He stuffed it into his blousy shirt. No one stopped him.

The chieftain indicated that he had made up his mind by swiftly turning around and barking an order to Kao, one of his trusted warriors. The rest of them followed Kao's lead as they headed into the forest again. The Tulus, guarded by another Khampa, were herded along from behind. Where they now found themselves was no wider than a rocky defile. Over rocks made smooth by the action of running water over many centuries they scampered along in the rear, with Kao and Hei-fu prodding and pushing them along to keep up. Thus they made their way until the cold winds of dusk whipped at their clothes. The long coats flapped; the skirts, least suitable for such a trip, billowed and fell. Terror drove the Tibetan Tulus at a faster pace, as they imagined that they now heard the demons of the peaks. The screeching drifted down the pine and fir trees. Theirs was a pace of anxious retreat that was taking on the dimensions of panic as they stared into bushes and treetops. The women and about three elders who had once been warriors began to lag noticeably behind. Open-mouthed and nostrils dilated, they gasped and kept moving the best they could. One of the women, the youngest, let out a sudden cry and fell behind. No one looked back. Another cry rent the air, and this time Hei-fu heard and looked around him fearfully. The other Khampas had gone ahead. He suddenly laughed aloud and forged on ahead, driving the others along the best he could.

It was week before the refugees came to Dzing Dzong. They heard a command – "Halt or we fire!" They didn't understand the words, but the command demanded obedience. The Khampas instinctively halted. Cautiously, with levelled rifles, they approached, but they could see nothing. All at once, from all directions, green clad riflemen of the Assamese Border Protection Force surrounded them. They were quickly disarmed and led to the base camp in Indian army trucks. About fifty jawans, Indian soldiers, turned out to see the Khampas. For the first time in more than a month, they were able to get a hearty meal.

The captain wasted no time. He immediately called up a thirteen hundred weight and three jeeps and took them into Tezpur for interrogation. The brown-coated Khampas got into the three jeeps. They followed in the wake of the truck in which the Tulus were put. A bluish haze covered their departure. Both the jeep and the thirteen hundred were under the control of the Assamese soldiers.

Tezpur was a town important for its proximity to the Tibetan border, from where the Indians were able to monitor the movements of border units of the Chinese army operating there to capture important elements of the Tibetan underground, who were putting up armed resistance against the occupation. Every group of itinerants were being treated as hostiles, rounded up, and sent to Lhasa. They wanted to clean up the borders between India and Nepal.

Tezpur stood close to the oil fields of India in this region, and that added to its importance. Nothing the Indian army could have done would have been of any strategic importance to them if China had wanted to take the oil fields, despite the thousands of Indian troops located in the state of Assam. The whole region was extremely vulnerable.

The outskirts of Tezpur were pitted with hundreds of tents in a wired-off perimeter. There was a ceaseless movement of men and vehicles and a hum of hundreds of voices. The truck drew up outside a large tent marked with a huge red cross in a white circle. The captain got out, slammed the door of the thirteen hundred weight shut, and striding into the tent, he herded the gypsies inside.

The Khampas stuck with the jeeps, poked at them, and examined some parts of the engines more with wonder than any understanding of the functions of what they reverently touched. Others stared at those inside the wired fenced-off area. Some of those within the enclosure called out to the curious newcomers. They were surprised when the Khampas replied. There was an excited jabbering from within and without as they recognized each other as Khampas. The bolder men and children came to the wires. It was then that the newcomers found out that their chieftain was no longer with them.

The Tulu women had to be dragged into the tent. They were wild-eyed and terrified. All Sam Dipp's attempts to reassure them were ignored. The men followed them into the tent, where they were all subjected to a medical examination and inoculated. They were then treated to some chappatis, Indian flat bread, and a vegetable brew. The hot victuals thawed their fears, and a new confidence began to spread across their faces and show in their eyes. The absence of the bullying Khampas was an added reassurance that their fate was improving and that for the first time they were safe because there was going to be some protection that they'd never enjoyed previously. The Khampas were taken to another section of the encampment, where they would be examined more closely because of their guerrilla capabilities. They were of greater value to the Indians. There was a definite plan for them in the near future.

The sun came out at last. It no longer struggled through a ceiling of thick mist, which had lifted. The temperature was rising slowly, and very welcome that was. It generated movement and liveliness in the camp. In the middle of the tents was a large wooden structure that raised its importance above the surrounding tents. Above it flew a large orange flag very much like a large sort of pennant. From within came the sound of low frequency chanting punctuated by the clanging of cymbals. Scattered all over the camp, or it could have become a refugee centre, perhaps, were over a thousand Tibetans, sad brownish groups. A few scattered utensils lay between them. Here and there were piles of clothing too. Children openly urinated near their holding groups without anyone doing anything to help them find toilets. Perhaps none had been provided. A few younger men had managed to scrounge warm khaki-coloured army pullovers and jeans. They moved with some authority from one group to another, instructing them in something. They seemed to be enjoying the authority that had obviously been invested in them.

Sam Dipp and his people were at a little distance from the other refugees. Sam Dipp and his friends still masticated the remains of their chappatis they had received. If any of them missed the unfortunate woman who had been taken from them by the Khampa on the way in, they betrayed no awareness or concern. The other women were still asleep on the grass. Their ordeals had been exhausting. It was with anxious eyes that Sam Dipp watched the Khampa chief and another, a stranger, weave in and out of the scattered throngs. The other man had similar mongoloid features as the Khampa chief. He cut an odd figure in his slippered feet, horn-rimmed spectacles, and felt hat. He wore a loose blousy grey gown. Spotting Sam Dipp from a distance, the Khampa and the stranger made their way to him. On the way, he spoke animatedly with the spectacled man, who blinked rapidly from time to time. He spoke to a soldier, a havildar, a non-commissioned officer also known a sergeant, who was called from nearby to assist.

"Yea admi ko ane do." It was a command to let Sam Dipp come to them.

The Khampa growled at the gypsy, into whose eyes fear flickered again. Two army jawans got Sam Dipp up and began to march him off as commanded by the havildar. The women who were lying down and resting got up and watched. Two Tulu men stopped eating. One threw his chappati down in disgust. The other picked it up and wolfed it down. Although Sam Dipp was flanked by two jawans, the chief himself had his arm in a vice-like grip. The grey-robed one and the Khampa kept up a mumbled conversation, with the grey-robed one shaking his head in denial of something. Sam Dipp placed all his hopes in him. The presence of the mild-mannered man brought him comfort.

Their pace had now slackened considerably, and then they halted. The elderly stranger kept suggesting something, and all the chief did by way of response was to continue a tirade of abuse at the Tulu, shaking him up whilst he did so.

"Cheat! Dog!"

The Khampa noticed that the stranger was pointing upwards and saying something. Above the tent, the Khampa saw an orange pennant flying, snapping as the wind whipped it about now and then. Inside, all was now quiet, none of the customary chanting and clanging of cymbals.

"Come on, gypsy thief," ground out the chieftain, propelling the Tulu into the tent.

Sam Dipp fell crashing inside and picked himself up gingerly. In a perfunctory manner, the Khampa clumsily copied the grey-robed one's obeisance, but all the while, he looked at the odd figure before them. On a wooden dais sat a very old and wizened priest who was fully covered in a deep plum-red robe. He wore a conical hat of rabbit fur, with blue beads embroidered around it. He was so old that he seemed asleep where he sat. All this had a strange effect on Sam Dipp, who was visibly frightened so much so that his teeth chattered as he looked from the old priest to the other serving monks around the dais. This was something he had never before encountered, and the presence of the Indian army soldiers and the barbed wire enclosures were more than he knew how to cope with.

The Khampa chieftain began to address the old man. "Holy man, blessed Lama Guchin Alwe …" As he paused, the monks broke off in the recitation of their office to stare. The grey-robed companion of the chieftain felt his bones jar as he landed on his back. Sam Dip had collided with him as he tore through the tent but got no farther than a few metres when the chieftain hurled himself at Sam Dipp and pinned him to the earth, his hunting knife held to his throat, where a thin red line came up with a trickle of blood. The execution would follow later, once they got him out of the territory controlled by the Indian army. The commotion brought a number of jawans running to the scene with their rifles at the ready. The grey-robed elderly one limped up to the entangled pair on the earth where they still lay.

It probably all looked uglier than it need have. It turned out that Sam Dipp, at best, was nothing more than a nuisance. He was the Tulu leader of a number of guerrillas who had carried out sporadic sabotage and ambushes on small Chinese patrols. He was on the lookout for a Tibetan who had gone over to the Chinese. He had been responsible for "buying" resistance leaders from tribals wherever they were available. Not every band of guerrillas were loyal Tibetans, and that was the trouble in many areas where the battle lines were forever changing. It led to a great deal of confusion, which played into Chinese hands. These tribal groups were thoroughly disorganized to be any effective united force against the Chinese. They jealously guarded their independence. Rumours had spread that the traitor was in the neighbourhood. Every group was hunting him down but not getting anywhere.

Moonlight played softly on the wide Brahmaputra plain. At Tezpur, it lent a touch of a strange glowing beauty on the army tents scattered about the place. It was not known whether the refugees were in any position to enjoy the aesthetics of the occasion or whether they, in their huddled groups, were too preoccupied with merely surviving. Night fires in braziers glowed like gigantic fireflies. The thirteen hundred weight and three jeeps reposed, dully gleaming like some prehistoric crustaceans. Most of the Khampas had fallen asleep in the jeeps, but Hei-fu and Kao noisily sipped steaming tea from canteens provided by the army. Every now and then, one or the other turned around to see if their chieftain was returning from the big tent.

In the big tent, the Khampa chieftain, happy to be wrapped in an army blanket, and the bespectacled interpreter were about to conclude their talks. For some reason, the elder chose to continue wearing his grey felt hat inside. Enfolded completely in his flowing warm grey robe, he sat on a stool. Sam Dipp dragged heavily on his lit *bedi* and made it glow and crackle. Bedi was uncured tobacco that the Indians used as a substitute for the cigarette.

"Yes, interpreter, I am sure," Sam Dipp emphasized. "Lama Guchin Alwe is dead, along with the two high priests from Shigatze. Yes, I can swear to it. I saw their bodies, their blood pouring out of them. My men and I tried to bring the corpses along to Tseun-Te, but on the way, a Chinese patrol ambushed us. I lost three men. More importantly, we lost three valuable rifles." The interpreter for the Indian army outpost rubbed his spectacles in his shawl to clean them. He coughed, turned, and spat to one side.

"The head lama from the Tsing-wan monastery isn't going to like our intrusion in his affairs very much. He is demanding to know why you were calling him Guchin Alwe," he laughed.

The Khampa threw a pebble into the night. These matters were of no concern to him. The god-king would hear about all this in good time. But he, in his mountain fastness, would not be worried. There were many more potentially deadly fears to keep his mind on survival of his kingdom and on as many of his people as possible. As long as chiefs like Sam Dipp managed to keep the passes open, they would receive the god-king's blessings, even if a few lamas here and there were inconvenienced or hurt in the process. This was why he could afford to shrug nonchalantly at what the interpreter had said.

"That Tulu dog, Sam Dipp, lied," said the chief. "I knew he lied. He only wanted to reach safety. He and his rats had wandered too far north of Dzing Dzong without knowing it and were in danger of being cut off in the mountains. It was there that we found them on our way to Tongla Pass."

The interpreter laughed softly because it turned out that the Khampa had been tricked by Sam Dipp, a Tulu, and had very nearly lost his life too.

"I had to bring them in," said the Khampa chief. "The Tulu dog lied. But there is a Chinese-trained traitor calling himself Guchin Alwe. He has led many revered leaders of our people fleeing their monasteries back into the hands of the Chinese, where they have been executed. This traitor, this cursed bastard, operates in the passes and knows the Khampa groups are helping these lamas to escape. For many weeks, I have watched out for this traitor to get a lead to him but have had no luck so far. He is a wily, cunning, and clever dog. But when I do …," he ground out between his teeth.

There was a sudden dull metallic flash in the tent light. The pale elder did not see from where the knife appeared, and the Khampa chieftain was gone. The interpreter shivered uncontrollably. For a while, there was no sound in the night. Suddenly, the grey-robed one felt his aloneness in the enveloping darkness around him and in the twinkling stars up above. Once again, he cleaned his spectacles, but this time to wipe the moisture from the night air off the lenses. He heard the jeeps start up, and then they were gone. He went out in time to see the last jeep load of Khampas roar away into the night. There had been no leave-taking, no niceties of farewells – just an urgency to get things done. No place for protocols.

Overhead, a tiny lump of clay around a rock ended its parabolic flight on the ground near where the jeeps had waited. The blanketed one stared at the place from where he thought it could have come. In the pale light of a waning moon, he saw the pallid hue of Sam Dipp's pinched face. He was peeping from behind the enclosure. It was his only token of defiance. And then he was gone, the night keeping his secret as best it could. From somewhere in the military outpost, a dog howled. The morning wasn't far away.

Tiger, Tiger!

The other day an old photograph, now brown with age and looking like a daguerreotype, fell out of an old photo album my wife was putting away. I was unaware of its existence. Mother had given the album to my wife. Over the years, it had remained concealed with a lot of bric-a-brac that we brought over to Australia when we arrived in 1967. It had been long forgotten ... until now. In it, I saw a small boy standing with a rifle much too big for a child. The boy was standing beside a large tiger that had been shot. That boy was I.

As I looked at it, I was lost temporarily in a flood of nostalgia. I saw more than a dead tiger. What came awash over me was a way of life I had enjoyed in British India, with its privileged existence. The romance of the past was important to me. It showed me all that came to be lost post- 1947. I remember a way of life that has no parallel.

My stepfather was an engineer for the East India Railway. He was a mail engine driver. His rank and salary enabled us to live a very comfortable and enjoyable life. He and his friends loved the wild life. They were products of the war that had just ended. They were able to own as many rifles and handguns as they liked. This led to the noble pastime of shikar, which means hunting, and more specifically what was called big game shooting, the dangerous art of hunting dangerous animals like elephants, tigers, and panthers in addition to wild boars and buffaloes. It didn't stop them from also bagging sambar, the large deer with a magnificent head of antlers. They also hunted the chinkara, the smaller deer that ran lightning fast, as we described it, when spooked, making them a most difficult target. Their venison was delicious and much sought after. Whenever we shot deer and or buffaloes, the natives got free fresh meat. Having no ice or refrigeration, we were never able to take home any of the meat. Home was a matter of some days away. This was why the villagers were overjoyed whenever we arrived. I wasn't always taken on these adventures with the shikaris, which disappointed me no end.

In our communities, we were always encouraged to buy guns – at first, air rifles, which were little more than harmless but good enough for hunting squirrels and doves.

On reflection, I would have to say that a prolonged life of war and seeing the terribly wounded arrive by train to military hospitals had its effect on growing sensibilities. From time to time, most of us lost loved ones in the battlefields or to bombings at home, which was then designated as Britain. How else can I explain my inordinate love for guns and shooting to wound or kill living creatures? At no time did I experience a twinge of conscience. It was a coming of age, a rite of passage. Today all this is considered anathema and a symbol of decadence – or worse, of inhumanity. I can assure you, to us in those heady days, the issues never arose. Conscience is fashioned by circumstance.

No more background stuff. On with the episode I had in mind: the tiger. My stepfather shot it from a low machan. More about this presently as my story unfolds.

Home was in a railway prescient in the town of Allahabad, in the state of Uttar Pradesh in India, should you want to look it up in an atlas out of curiosity. Dad and his circle of six friends and their families were very close. Dad and his friends, and even some wives, loved the lure of the thick Indian jungles where wild animals roamed. We often went on weekend picnics.

Makundi was about four hundred kilometres away. To get there, we had to persuade a friendly engine driver and guard to let us travel with all our gear and servants, whom we needed to pitch our tents and cook and carry. The servants always looked out for the events. The slow-moving goods train usually took about two days, after which, at a designated spot, the train would be pulled up to where a couple of bullock carts would be waiting with the usual quota of village men to help us off the train and onto the carts. Then the goods train pulled away to continue its journey, with friendly waves from the train driver and guard with whom we had lived briefly during the trip. The whole organization was always in the hands of a friendly forest ranger, Ahmad, whose job was the protection of wild animals and spotting fires – and being obliging for the sake of a few hundreds rupees.

It took over four hours of a rough bone-wracking journey home, which turned out to be the forest ranger's bungalow in the middle of a clearing a couple of kilometres from the village of Makundi, population of about forty or fifty, most of whom were Muslim farmers and growers of mango trees.

We spent the first day getting the travel fatigue out of our system. Dad and Dan Goncalves, a Portuguese Indian railway driver, the most dedicated of hunters, went to the village in the afternoon and hired the headman and three others to find the best place to attract tigers and build a machan. Dad said later that it took them an hour before they found the most likely spot. It was an old leafy tree with spreading limbs. The men quickly cut enough sturdy cross branches and hammered out a high platform which could accommodate three men. That is what a machan is – a sort of platform built above the forest floor at a safe height that a tiger would not be able to reach but that could still offer a safe and clear shot at the animal. Dad and Dan climbed up, tried it out, and were quickly satisfied that it was what they wanted. They trudged back to the village and paid off the hired hands, who returned sweeping salaams, obviously delighted with the money.

On the third day, excited villagers came running. They were exhausting themselves. Their breathing was laboured.

"Shere Khan! Shere Khan!" they screamed with fear and excitement, which meant "Tiger! Tiger!"

Shere Khan (a name given to the noble animal as a mark of respect born out of a natural fear of it) had been spotted making its way back to the area it had previously left for another part of the forest where it had made a kill: a baby baboon. It was returning to its other territory now. So arrangements were made. Dad decided he would need to use his most powerful rifle, and he asked me to fetch it from the bedroom. I brought the Italian 423 to him, trembling with excitement. Dad noticed it. He thought for a while and said to me, "Rob, feel like coming along with us? Won't get scared? One wrong move and you will scare it away and we may never find it again. It will be gone to its other hunting grounds. It's a bit risky, but—"

He turned to Dan and asked his opinion. Dan looked at me, and I knew he didn't want to disappoint me. He smiled and ruffled my hair, saying, "Why ever not? His mother will want to kill me when she finds out but what the hell … It could be the experience Rob needs to get him started."

Get him started! I felt myself growing into a hunter, a shikari. I was soon walking tall. Wait until the other guys heard of this. They'd be jealous as hell. I drew a deep breath and swelled up with manly pride.

"I promise you, Dad, I won't disappoint you. I know I will learn a lot from this," I replied, giving him the biggest hug I could. Dan gave me a playful punch on my arm as a sign of acceptance.

I couldn't wait for the sun to go down on that all-important fourth day. It seemed to take forever. Whilst the light was strong enough, the three of us headed off to the tree that had been previously selected as the killing tree. Along with us went a small goat in tow, one that the headman had sold us. It was to be the bait. Dad carried it to the tree to which it was tied. It had been partly sedated to prevent it crying out. Some hay was scattered near it should it feel hungry anytime during the night.

We made ourselves comfortable. Being early summer, it wasn't really cold, but Dad rugged me up anyway. Fear has a way of generating its own chill. He made me comfortable and told me I could sleep if I wanted. He would let me know when the tiger came. As if I could sleep! So the night set in.

The darkness in the forest is so final. It claims all living things. Nothing prevails over the primeval fears it generates at the hint of approaching death.

I listened to the croaking of the crickets and a chorus of bullfrogs around the tree we sat in – we, strange predatory un-winged creatures that the forest did not claim as its own. I felt we were also violating a law of the jungle. Here was no killing for food and survival; it was a response to a disguised lust for killing that was masked as sport. We were outsiders and had no business there. Life was being contaminated.

In the dark of the forest night, you hear all sorts of strange noises and finally make out one that is the sound of your heart pounding in your ears and temple. Suddenly, my train of consciousness was interrupted. The goat bleated. It was a cry for its life. It bleated again. Dad nudged me gently. I nudged him back to let him know I was awake. Dan slowly lifted the rifle and passed it to Dad. The silence picked up a throbbing that was the pulse of fear and excitement. Dad took a deep breath. Below us, the bushes swished gently. The goat strained at its leash and jumped about to get free, bleating piteously as it did so. It clearly sensed that it had such a short time left to live. It knew its death was at hand.

Below us, I saw the long sinuous form of the animal. I heard its strenuous breathing as it gathered its primeval energy to attack. I smelt the tiger from where I sat. It was all happening in such deliciously slow motion, as it were. I was afraid to breathe hard in case it heard me.

Then the forest sprang to life. Dad had switched on the headlight attached to the 423. Bright light washed over the night world. Every leaf and branch of every bush below sprang into view. The lord of the forest snarled, crouched threateningly, stared into the stabbing light, and was rooted to the spot, unable to move, unable to save itself. At that moment, the prospect of a nocturnal meal was surely the furthest thing from its mind. It snarled in both defiance and fear. It must have felt itself in a situation over which it could not exercise any control, let alone its accustomed mastery. It must have sensed its death. Its eyes glowed a sharp green. Its bared teeth hurled out a pathetic defiance and a threat of death.

It roared in anger as it sensed a trap. It roared again, and the goat bleated several times. This was an opera as old as the ancient forest itself. It was the theatre of death. The tiger roared again. The next roar was the roar of Dad's 423. The bullet raced like a streak of lightning into the skull from between its two beautiful eyes. My heart broke for the poor creature, once lord of all, now a potential rug in the centre of our living room. I knew then that I would never, ever again contemplate being a wild game hunter. The moment informed me of my contemptible meanness. But it had become a defining moment, a time of self-discovery. I wondered long afterwards how Dad and Dan, grown men, had faced this crisis and turned out to be the hunters that they were with no qualms, no moral hangovers to worry them. Then I thought of wars and the dreadful one that we had only recently come through, with its massive loss of life and destruction of cities. I found it all too complex for my small mind to deal with.

The tiger did not twitch during the dying that came to it so swiftly. The little goat had thoroughly exhausted itself and collapsed. In reality, it had died. Dad said its fear had been so powerful that its tiny heart could not bear the pressure anymore. The only two who were happy that night were Dad and Dan, who congratulated each other, so deliriously drunk with the victory of the gun that they failed to notice me in my sudden silence and confusion.

Soon the dawn came. The villagers arrived early. They cheered and danced madly. The village would be celebrating the night away. Soon they had trussed the dead tiger to a large pole, and they began chanting. The headman thanked us for killing off the predator that had been taking a heavy toll on its cattle and goats. It had also killed a child who had strayed unsupervised into the forest one day. A villager from another village had been visiting and had belatedly made a foolish attempt to return to his own village.

The bullock carts were loaded up again when the shikar was over, and the visit ended. As we made our way out of the forest that morning, the children of the village, cheering and singing, ran along behind the cart for a short distance before running home again. The devil had been killed and they would be safe now. Mine was only then starting to come alive.

What Does She Want?

The two women stood at the drawn curtains and peered out cautiously every now and then. The motherly one held the younger woman back, carefully shielding her. They were more than merely curious. They watched a man and woman across the road. They were heavily coated against the crisp, cold early Parisian spring. A lively wind was making life miserable for the early pedestrians. Rain drove shoppers in and out of shops. Umbrellas were turned inside out when the gusts got strong enough to become a nuisance. Dead leaves danced crazily before the sweeping winds. It wasn't the best of the season; it wasn't the worst.

"Your father is never around when he's most needed. I think I'll get your cousin, Mahmud, to take a look at these two," the elder of the two women said.

She felt more than a little bit apprehensive. It was the duty of the men to provide the family its security and protection. The past was forever just around the corner. There were days when she was convinced they should never have done anything about having a girl. The way they had gone about it was wrong, surely, but it wasn't her duty or her place to speak her mind.

They peered out again. The couple still stood out there in the cold. The man was stamping his feet to keep warm. The woman looked as pale as a *bhoot*, a ghost or devil, her hair limp and straggly. She stood still as a statue. Her breathing was ending in a wheezing.

"What does she want?" asked the young woman.

"You say this isn't the first time you've seen her. Tell me more about her," said Zainab, the mother. "Has she threatened you in any way? Do you think she's a thief?"

The young woman looked out again. There was a lot that had been happening which she couldn't understand but found intriguing. She seemed to take a long time before replying.

"No. I don't find her threatening, strangely enough. Sad and weird, yes. The first time I saw her was when I was leaving the Sorbonne, having done my research, and was looking for a taxi at the Rue De Madeline taxi rank. She let out a gasp when she saw me and seemed to put out a hand as if begging, which she obviously was too well dressed to be doing. I'm not sure exactly what it was that I saw."

She turned to face her mother. "Oddly enough, she seemed as if she wanted to be friendly … Strange, is it not? I think she was mistakenly thinking that she knew me."

The mother snorted and moved towards the other room. She called out to Mahmud, who silently and respectfully entered with the day's *Le Figaro* in hand. He tried to look stern but couldn't help smiling at Halifa.

"Let this be proof of what we say when we insist that you go into the burqa, for it is the only means of protecting the integrity and purity of Muslim women," the mother said firmly. "Now you have seen for yourself what we mean. So no more of your liberal Western cultural demands, young lady. The university is no place for our women, I've always maintained. Your father has been completely negligent. Things are going to change from now on or back you go to Fez. Mahmud, come listen to Halifa's story."

The elderly man was greying at the temples. He had a stately deportment. He came in and stood looking at the younger woman with a gentle chiding look that was mildly amused at the same time. He extended his hand and held her shoulder with a fondness of a father. The younger woman was encouraged enough to look into his eyes innocently.

"When I saw her again, her eyes were watery. She seemed to appeal to me silently, as if she wanted to ask me something. This was last week, when Mumtaz and I were shopping in Plas de La Concorde. We hurried away, Mumtaz giggling as she always does."

Mahmud came to the curtain and looked out into the street. He looked around slowly, covering every possible angle. He was cautious but not alarmed. He stood peeping out at the Parisian world which was so different from their own world, but he found it quite charming in its own way. Blending two diverse cultures was no easy task.

"What does she want?" he asked.

"I don't know," was the reply.

"I'll go out and find out, shall I?" he said as he left for the street. The women made no move to restrain him. They had no idea how this could be done without offending the person approached. It smattered of a certain arrogance.

The younger woman seemed indifferent to the drama building up. Besides, there was work to do. There was that assignment on the psychology lecture that she missed when she had a cold last week. She would need to download the talk. Mumtaz was sure to have the lecture. She was much more assiduous than she was. She admired Mumtaz for this. But it got tiresome when her parents kept holding her up as an example of something she should be emulating. She hated poor Mumtaz in those moments, though she realised it wasn't her fault.

"The last time I saw her was yesterday, when I was leaving the library. As I passed her, I heard her softly and uncertainly call after me."

"What did she say, Halifa?" asked her mother.

"Something that made no sense then and even less now. It sounded like Mattie or … Maddie … or something like that."

The two looked at each other. "Surely not Madeleine," whispered the mother, a look of some concern in her grey eyes. Here was an imminent threat.

"Madeleine? No. It didn't sound like Madeleine. But why do you say 'Madeleine'? What does that mean?" asked Halifa.

The elder woman's face was drained of colour by now, and a look of a secret fear came into her eyes as she drew in a rasping breath.

After about half an hour, Mahmud returned. He went to Halifa and looked deeply into her eyes. He slowly shook his head and said that nothing below seemed to be a problem to him. He led her into his office. He spoke at length about seeing things and imagining problematic situations. These were normal for many who may have special intuitive powers and maybe she, Halifa, was one of these. She should feel free to share them with her parents anytime. They would surely be glad to think things through with her. For that matter, so would he.

Halifa suddenly beamed a wonderful smile at her cousin. "Of course. Thank you, Mahmud. I most certainly will. I shall remember that next time."

She turned to go, feeling quite sure that there would be other such times. She secretly hoped she could come across the strange apparition, who may not be such a strange apparition. In fact, it may not be an apparition at all. "Apparition" wasn't a word she was comfortable with in such an experience.

Adam's Apple

Bayshore High School was on the boundary between the wealthy suburb of Claremont and the working-class areas of Mosman Bay. That was just the problem for the Baker family, as we came to find out.

I had a year more to spend in Australia before my visa expired, so I applied for a teaching post in the school that lay a couple of kilometres from where I lived in a leased apartment in a small block of flats, which I shared with Somalis, Filipinos, Scots, and mostly Australians who had come from other parts of the country. This was due to the FIFO (fly-in fly-out) syndrome.

It was apparent that in the drive to update the renovation program and put more resources into West Australian schools, Bayshore must have been a low priority. Rumour had it that it was to be closed down, and the students were to be relocated in another part of Mosman Bay community, which was farther away from the gentrified Claremont.

I walked down every morning to the school to share the way to school with those who also lived close by. I came to know a number of Somalis and Filipinos who, in the beginning, were shy and reluctant to keep me company and talk freely, but later they became more sociable and even quite friendly. I came to learn a lot about their families and the problems that had become parts of their life. I learnt something about multiculturalism in Australia.

I was given a class of thirty-five students who seemed to have been part of an overt policy of socio-economic segregation. I told myself not to start looking for problems. In the year I had left, I should try to enjoy the remaining experiences rather than start looking for trouble.

I took the 503 bus every morning and later that afternoon. This gave me closer ties with many Bayshore kids, who lugged ponderous school bags into the narrow spaces provided for passengers. The little ones found it more than a little exerting and stumbled into their seats perspiring, puffing, and panting from their efforts, especially during the hot summer days. Somehow it brought me near Abu, the black little Somali, who I suspected made it his business to get a seat near me. He often kept a place near him vacant and with a big Somali smile would invite me to sit there. No one in Bayshore smiled like him. His was so genuine that it had no comparison. We struck up a closeness that year, and when I left Australia for home at the end of the year, he saw me off at the airport with his family of six other siblings and parents. I found the farewell very touching.

However, the story isn't about Abu but about a little urchin who broke my heart. I wouldn't be surprised if it touched yours too. His name was Adam Baker. I thought he really wasn't ready for his first year of secondary education, though he was old enough, but he had to be moved along with the herd because he was the same age.

He must have been smaller than Abu, but he had a much bigger skull, and that gave him a strange appearance, I have to say. He was very pale and thin. I would call him gaunt. He was one of my thirty-five who managed to squeeze into the room allocated to us. I thought surely no one could possibly survive in that room, especially not in the forty-degree heat we often got in the summer sessions.

I didn't so much have to keep an eye on the poor soul as deal with the way he demanded my attention. He rarely did any work. His handwriting hadn't formed fully as of yet. It looked like a spider's scrawl. His exercise books looked consumptive because he insisted on pulling out pages and making darts. Instead of punishing him, I would try to talk sense into his thin skull. All to no avail. He didn't seem to have the energy to do anything. I intended to bring it to the attention of the school nurse.

There were days when the schoolyard became a battlefield at times, with apples, oranges, and bananas used as missiles. I had no idea what started the assaults, nor did any other teachers. Staff meetings were held to find a solution, but the results were no different. Individuals who had the misfortune to be caught in the act were individually dealt with. Those caught in groups had to stay back after school hours to clean up until protesting parents aborted the intended deterrent. The kids won every time. Then a lull would fall for some reason and sanity returned. For a time. It seemed that every season there had to be at least three if not more such ballistic sessions. Twice it fell on my yard duty, and I was hit both times, much to the amusement of my first years. I got my own back once when a more enterprising militant tried to race past me with a pocket full of eggs. I put out my hand, and his shirt was soon splattered with egg. "Hell, what did you have to do that for?" he yelped with disgust at his state. I had to laugh that time.

What did any of this have to do with Adam?

I began to notice that after class resumed after lunch and everyone was seated and working maths problems, he would ask to go to the toilet. I had to ask him why he hadn't been during recess. Each time, I threatened it was the last time he was being allowed. His pale, drawn face would reveal genuine distress. On one such occasion, I pulled his bluff, and when he asked to be allowed to go to the toilet, I let him go; but a few minutes later, I crept out of the classroom, leaving the rest of the class busy problem solving. I was about to do a bit of my own problem solving that day. It was too much of a mystery, one I had to come to grips with somehow.

At first, I couldn't see him anywhere, but just as I was beginning to give up hope, I spotted him behind the school shop, which had closed for the day, the staff gone home. He sat with his back to a plane tree with two Granny Smiths near him as he hungrily bit into another. My heart broke when I saw this, and when he stopped chewing, I felt like an intruder as he turned pained, embarrassed, and scared eyes of a cornered rabbit on me … and the poor wretch even apologized.

In a flash, the sad social truth dawned on me. Adam was having the only lunch he'd get that day. How long had this been going on? And why couldn't he bring his own lunch to school as the others did? His lunch had to be the apples he found scattered about the school oval, the missiles of the usual apple fights. His parents never gave him any lunch. He began to cry just then. Instinctively, I knelt by him and held his head in my arms. It was the only thing I was able to do – and the only way I could hold back my own tears. I smiled at him and tried to reassure him that it was OK. I said as much and added that he hadn't done anything wrong and that he wasn't in trouble but he had to accompany me to see the nurse. The poor little fellow decided to take his Granny Smiths along. He wasn't going to give them up to anybody.

In a flash, I recognized instinctively that here was a tragedy beyond me. My authority did not extend beyond the four rooms of the classroom. The school nurse and child protection had to be called in immediately.

When the period bell rang and the students all filed out to their other subject rooms, I took Adam with me to see Mrs Dobbs, who just happened to be leaving. I was relieved to catch her in time. Mrs Dobbs was a compassionate and efficient nurse. She invited me into her office and took over. I'm grateful I could not stay, for I had other classes that needed my attention. However, that day I could not concentrate for the remaining periods. God knows what I taught or how I got through the rest of the day.

Mrs Dobbs met me next day and asked if I could spare her a few minutes of my time, which I gladly did. Adam hadn't been getting lunch for some time now, nor had he been given money to buy his own. His father's "woman" hated him and made him sleep in the garage. His father couldn't be bothered with him because the woman bossed him about all day. He was too scared of her and just didn't want a scene. Adam soon found that not only wasn't he welcome in the house but that the woman also changed all the locks. He couldn't even get in for a shower or to get a change of clothing.

He didn't return to school for the rest of the year, but it was time for me to leave Australia, as my visa had nearly expired. Before I left Bayshore, little Abu, my friendly little Somali, timidly sidled up to me and shyly asked me to write to him sometime. His manner was diffident and hesitant, suggesting I would likely reject his overture. He wanted to tell me how things were progressing in school. I thought it was a good idea. I knew in my heart that this little Somali was going places and had a wonderful future, and yes, I would like to keep in touch with him. We exchanged addresses.

That was how one day I got a letter from little Abu that burned a hole in my heart. Poor little Adam took his own life. He was crossing Canning Highway in Melville when he saw a huge Mack truck bearing down on him. He threw himself in its way and died on impact. The school didn't know about it because by then Child Welfare (there's a misnomer if ever there was one!) had withdrawn Adam and placed him with a caregiver in a house that had six other similarly unwanted and unloved children. Abu had tried to keep in touch with him, but it wasn't what Adam, the loveless and restive one, wanted. He had been unable to pull out of the downhill run he was on. Obviously, there came a time when a sensitive child like Adam had decided he had had enough.

Little Abu managed to write a fairly long letter, giving me the news about his family and some things about Bayview. Abu was doing very well, and his letter showed the confidence he was acquiring. Before he ended, he gave me a few details about Adam.

I shall never forget some of his words. He had tried to make a friend of Adam, but from what I could judge, he wasn't very successful. Before he ended his letter, he wrote, "You know, sir, Adam was a very sad boy. He really wasn't that bad. He was just badly hurt. His father did not like him."

No school psychologist seemed to have picked that up, I thought, but little Abu had an insight that was priceless. Out of the mouths of babes, et cetera. You know the old Biblical saying. Oh so true.

No, Adam was not a bad boy. The words made my blood boil, thinking of those who had inflicted such injuries on the defenceless little boy who had spent his short life looking for love. My narrative really began the day I first went looking for someone I mistakenly thought was a time waster and found that all he wanted was something to eat. His hunger had led him to look for his apple for lunch. I found myself wondering whether his death was the only real break in life he got. He must have thought so too.

Black Turban

Three of us sat in a room. It was bare except for its white carpeted floor. Someone had brought the three cushioned chairs in for us. I noticed that there were no windows, just the door through which we had entered and through which we would leave the mosque. It was loosely called the New Mosque, which was attended cautiously by some Muslims who favoured modernity and moderation.

There was an agelessness about the newly arrived scholarly Imam Akbar Khan that graced his small greying well-kept beard and smiling intense blue eyes. He sat looking at us in silence for a long time. I knew patience was going to be needed – that and the need to cooperate. I was an outsider here and felt every bit like one. I'd take my cue from the imam. There was an indefinable quality about him, one I couldn't be sure of. There was holiness hidden under a sort of tired humanity. It was a strange amalgam.

He leaned forward in his chair, and looking at Farad all the time he spoke, his voice was as soft as a whisper floating in from afar. I saw Farad shift in his seat, and I wondered if he was a bit uncomfortable under the imam's stare.

"You asked to see me, Farad."

I wasn't sure whether it was a question or a gentle statement. The way he spoke the lad's name suggested that he wanted to be alone with him. As a mark of respect, I rose and bowed to excuse myself. Privacy was going to be essential at such a time. I knew Farad wanted me there, but I was more concerned about doing the right thing in the eyes of the imam. The imam immediately held out his hand to stop me.

"Please. I'd like you to be present, Mr. Meier, if you don't mind," he said without looking at me.

I sat back in my cushioned seat and exchanged glances with Farad, who I knew needed a measure of reassurance. We'd been over his story many times previously and had come to the point that now the story must be told to someone in authority, to a man like Imam Akbar Khan, the recently installed imam who'd come from the newly formed Centre of Islamic International, London.

It was in not so much the silence as it was in the stillness of the room when Farad's youthful story was told in a controlled but not emotionless voice. I will not tell that full story here. It is sufficient that you get just enough to give you an idea of the waste, the destitution, the tragedy of his life. In the story of Farad, you will come to know the story of his entire race, of the brave Hazzara people of North eastern Afghanistan, who, looked upon as dogs and a source of impurity by the Pashtun majority, had suffered, throughout their history, rejection and racial persecution and all the injustices that followed from it.

He was only eight when he saw the pick-up trucks arrive in the village. Firing shook the air. People screamed and ran. Farad saw his mother and sisters raped by men whilst his father was held down and made to watch. Mercifully, he was then shot in the head. The boy saw all this from where he was hidden behind straw bales and blankets. Houses began to burn, but for some reason, his was forgotten or the fire hadn't caught on. We will never know. The quiet litany of woes drifted on and on, punctuated by stifled sobs. Farad wiped his eyes once or twice.

What fascinated me was the interplay of the emotions of the two characters. These emotions, I knew, were too deep for any outsider like me to ever feel or understand. The imam was now leaning far forward, his elbows on his knees, his face between his hands. Somewhere in the space between the two, I seemed to sense a meeting of two kindred spirits. I'll say no more about this because it was too easy for me to get carried away and say things that would sound all wrong when I tried to talk about them later.

The imam had straightened in his seat and so had Farad. I felt out of place. I didn't know what to do with my hands or where to look. We sat for a while like that. The Imam broke the silence. "Is there more to the story, Farad?" he asked.

The lad glanced at me and nodded. "Yes, Imam Akbar Khan. There is," he said in a whisper. "Recently I have seen the leader of the Taliban troop who did this thing to my parents, brothers, and sisters. I know where he lives too."

The imam's eyebrows lifted almost imperceptibly. His frail hands shook. He was clearly disturbed. His eyes blinked a few times and what seemed like tears filled them. The imam nodded encouragement.

"I was across a street one evening when I saw him dressed like the Taliban, even wearing his black turban as he played with his grandson in his back garden. When he looked my way, he seemed puzzled and slowly put the boy down and went inside. I saw him peering through the curtains of his daughter's kitchen. I went home. There was nothing I could do. I felt like such a coward."

Imam Akbar Khan put one hand on the lad's shoulder and the other on mine. "No. Not a coward. You are a Hazzara. You have the courage and the spirit of the Hazzara. What is happening here today, in this room, at this moment, Farad and Mr Meier, is the way forward for all our peoples. This is what the Abrahamic Alliance must give the new world now. This might well be the last chance that our peoples will have. Farad, thank you for your inestimable gift. I owe you, and I will repay. Maybe not now, but you can rest assured that I will. Allah Bis'millah," he whispered, walking us to the only door. As in life, there is only that one door through which we come and through which we leave one day.

We blinked in the brightness of what felt like a new day. Once in my car again, we drove to the house he shared with some other Hazzara family, who came running to meet us and asked Farad where he'd been. Farad turned to thank me for the lift and smiled at their curiosity.

He walked with me to my car. He was quiet. I stopped with my hand on the car door. I couldn't leave just yet. I was burning to ask the question to which I must have the answer and without which I would forever be curious and disappointed.

I paused, hand on the door, not knowing what was to follow.

"Is that all, Farad? Nothing more? That swine is to escape justice. No court in Australia would be likely to do anything, I'm afraid. We can move to get his visa cancelled."

Farad looked at the earth silently. He raised his eyes to fasten them on mine. A small smile played about his lips, and he shook his head.

"I suppose the appropriate and traditional Hazzarra response would be to kill him … slowly," I said. "In the Afghan wilderness, this would be natural justice. But that is what we have fled from. None of my people would really want that anymore. It would be dragging the ugliness of our culture here with us. We have learnt that we have to be better than such animals. But don't worry – the imam knows what must be done. His continued presence in this country would pollute Australia. Come back a year from now. Let us see what has been done. Sharia works in more ways than one. It is a much older justice system than secular democratically devised laws and has a longer and far-reaching effect that is cleansing."

He laughed quietly and rested a hand on my shoulder. He thanked me for my concerns and said he felt that he now had a brother here in this foreign land.

I drove back the way we had come. I pulled up in a quiet lane outside the house where we had seen the black-turbaned

Taliban murderer. There had to be a way we could get justice for the murdered people. I couldn't share Farad's cool and apparent dispassionate response. I hated these radical extremists whose hands were tainted with the blood of innocent people. He came out just then to pick up the toys with which he and the boy had been playing. He was playing a different role nowadays, but beneath that feigned domestic face was one whose blood could soon boil over, whose pleasant life here could just as easily be transformed into the bestial nature that had been his for most of his life in Afghanistan. I wondered how he had managed to find his way through the labyrinth of security checks in place. I imagine he had important contacts in important places. Intimidation and bribery were the usual ways of getting results in a corrupt government hierarchy, and this monster would have known how to manipulate both methods. Now he was here in Australia, where he might very well be a sleeper. I wondered how I could alert someone in authority of the danger we now faced. The war in Afghanistan was reaching down into the very heart of my country.

He saw me as he was picking up the little boy, and he gave me a smile, displaying wide-gapped and crooked teeth. A primitive evil lurked there as clear as daylight, but I was unable to do anything about it. I knew what I longed to do. Before he disappeared behind the fly-wired backyard security door, he turned around once more and let me have another mocking smile.

Cleansing the Land

They came early in the morning, just after sunrise. They had three trucks that had seen better days, and they must have had a lot of trouble keeping them on the road. Smoke billowed from the rear of them as they bobbed and bounced on the rough country road that connected the village to the main road that led to Vlastograd, on the River Grava. Behind the trucks came a four-wheel-drive BMW that was of more recent vintage. They were feared through the length and breadth of the land. No one could see who sat in front because the windows were heavily tinted, as were all military and paramilitary vehicles.

Our little village stood at the base of the foothills and a couple of kilometres from the River Grava, which provided water for our fifteen homes; a derelict mosque, if one can call it that; and small pastures. Life was always very hard here. Men, women, and children had to force the land to yield a living, working from sunrise to sunset. Our produce was taken some thirty kilometres to market for whatever it could fetch. It was a hostile market that offered us only a part of what others could get. Yacob Osman was our headman, and we trusted him to get us the best prices he could. He did his best for all of the mixed community. We lived together in harmony and respect for each other.

From what I dimly remember, and told the KFOR officials later, it was Yacob and his two eldest sons who arrived to enquire what the newcomers needed. We lived through tragic and violent times, so we had to be cautious about strangers. Near the bonnet of the BMW stood two men. A short distance away stood about ten others who looked to me like soldiers, but they belonged to the political arm of the police.

Yacob approached the fat man, who was dressed in battle fatigues and a matching peak cap on which nested his Polaroids. He had a riding crop in one hand and the other was on his hip. He was an imposing figure from whom emanated a cruel authority. The other man was a wizened old black-robed priest who also wore a black stove-type sort of hat that was flattened at the top. The priest held a large map on which the fat man with his riding crop was pointing to the houses in our little village. Grouped around the leading truck were about a dozen paramilitary personnel with automatic weapons drawn. The officer and the priest ignored Yacob at first – until our headman came abreast and greeted them obsequiously.

I had just come out of our house and was starting to feed grain to our few hens and chicks when I saw what was the first of the darkest and final day in our village life. They spoke together briefly in a manner that made Yacob hold out his hands beseechingly, only to be rudely brushed aside. It made him and his two eldest turn away and scuttle back to their own house, which was the farthest in the village but close to the mosque. He cried out to his other sons as he went. His sons came running out to meet their father. The little ones were also running after them to find out what the clamour was all about.

They came to our house first because we were the nearest. Orders were barked at the soldiers, which sent them running into our house to my father, Ivan; grandfather, Yusef; and my brothers, Abu and Osip. Grandfather must have been a hothead in his time. He did what no one else dared to do. He stood in the doorway with arms outstretched to deny the armed intruders access. They cast him to the ground and kicked his frail body out of the way. Ivan was just in time to hold his sons off. He shouted at them angrily, but it didn't stop the men from spending time beating and kicking them.

Mother then burst into the room where all this was happening and on her knees implored the soldiers to spare her sons. They managed to pick themselves up off the ground and go protect her. They formed a barrier that father joined. I remember falling off the steps of the back veranda and hiding under the house, shaking all over and biting my lips to keep from crying. I was too terrified to think clearly. After all, I was only fifteen and had heard what they were doing to young women and girls. What could I have done? All I knew was naked fear that paralyzed me. I was never able to get rid of the guilt that overcame me that fateful day.

I didn't see them haul all of them out to the trucks. The men were ordered into the second, whilst Mother went ino the leading truck. One of the soldiers saw me and dragged me to be with my mother, who grabbed me in her arms and begged me to be a good girl and to be quiet. It was only then that mother discovered other women and children cowering inside. Three large women in uniform kept watch over them. The keening of the captive women drew abuse from the guards, who yelled at them to shut it. I could see what was happening. All our belongings were being thrown out and heaped in a pile.

The trucks then rolled to the next house. The Abrahamoffs were all outside and wailing. The men had seized pickaxes and shovels in a bid to fight for their homes. The village had been a peaceful settlement in which no arms were allowed. The trucks halted, and the armed men ran out. One of them fired a brief burst of his machine gun, and one of the sons fell dead. At shouted commands, the other men raised their hands in surrender. The father couldn't keep his eyes away from the body of the bloodied and fallen son. He kept calling his name, but to no avail. The inert body failed to respond. To forestall any further act of armed resistance, the soldiers handcuffed them and threw them into the truck, where other men crouched in fear. The captives kept calling for justice and forgiveness. They offered their services for anything the soldiers wanted them to do. They kept asking after their loved ones in the other truck.

The best part of the morning went, turning other villagers out of their homes and loading them onto the trucks that were now quite full. It was doomsday for all.

They left the mosque for last. All the religious material was piled up in a heap. They didn't find much to add to the growing piles outside. They left the old imam for last. Nearly every soldier beat him. Not a bone could have been left intact; he was so battered and bleeding profusely. He must have died before they shot him several times.

After the last house had been ransacked, the old black-robed priest emerged from the interior of the black four-wheel-drive BMW with a phial and sensor from which he coaxed a plume of black smoke and a smell of incense. He swung the sensor about in all directions as the soldiers knelt as if in mass. This was the ritual of purgation that was being enacted everywhere they went. The land was being cleansed, purged of the stain of the Ottoman pollution. History was being reversed, or so it was claimed.

From the trucks, a loud wailing broke out that the authorities failed to silence, despite their threats of further violence. The men and women saw columns of smoke rise from the piles of their belongings. All that had made up what were homes for them, all that had been bought or made and been cherished for all those years, was now being reduced to rubble and ash. Where there had been love, shelter, and means of livelihood, everything went up in smoke. Their lives were being brutally rubbed out, extinguished forever.

Flames were devouring mattresses, bed linens, chairs, and tables. All that had been once part of rich and vibrant families was gone forever. Flames curled around the cradles, and soon they were reduced to cinders, as were innocence and love. The sound of flames crackling mixed with the desperate and grief-stricken cries from within the trucks made a sickening cacophony of the gruesome tragedy under Balkan skies that were beginning to cloud up with a promise of rain that would have been a boon for the small pastures that were now destined for destitution. The cattle and sheep had been driven off – to be rounded up later by some thieving Serbs, no doubt.

The officer had lowered his Polaroids to mask his face and give anonymity to the acts of evil. He strode off to the leading truck that bore the women and children and gave the driver his orders. Some woman must have asked him something, but his only reply was a torrent of abuse. He nodded at the driver, who let in the clutch and began the trip to the given destination, no doubt a detention centre somewhere.

He tramped back to the second truck with a map and gave more orders. Those in the truck began frantically screaming and asking where they were being taken. All the answer they got was the shouting of a single word that was later to resound around the world. With an outstretched arm, the officer pointed to the horizon and shouted, "Srebrenitsa!"

Eating Watermelon on the Cappuccino Strip

"Nigel!"

From the ruck of disembarking passengers who had just arrived from Bundaberg, he heard his name called. He saw the wave of her hand and her smiling and radiant face. She had endured a two-hour delay because the plane had been delayed at Alice Spring because of an engine problem.

They had spent the last three years apart, he in Bundaberg, where he taught, and she at the veterinary college in Murdoch University. They met during their holidays. It had been proving expensive, but they had known it would from the start. He had insisted that she finish her vet studies, and then she could return and be reunited with him, nevermore to part. Their future would be more secure with her practising as a vet.

"I have something rather special to say to you, my Tammy," he whispered, so softly that she barely heard him.

"Tell me. You must tell me!" she cooed happily, but as often as she urged him to, he would not.

"No, you must wait," he responded. "I will when the time comes."

After he had embraced her and they had kissed happily, they went to the carousel, where he picked up his luggage, and then she led him out to the car park where her old VW was parked under the gum trees on the periphery, the only place she was able to find a parking space. As much as her importunity grew, so did his negative mood, so Tammy decided that it would be best not to spoil anything. When the time came, he would tell her the secret. She refused to conjecture what it might be.

Fifty or so minutes later, she was opening the door of her flat. They kissed happily again. She asked if he was hungry. He was, adding that sleep would be very welcome. He had had a tiring run, and some kip wouldn't do any harm.

Tammy quickly phoned all her friends with the good news. She couldn't keep the excitement out of her voice. The Smiths invited them to dinner the next day. The church group planned a picnic to welcome Nigel, for they had met him and enjoyed doing things together with the pair whenever he came to Perth.

Tammy loved cooking his favourite dishes for him when they decided to stay in and eat instead of eating out, which was what they loved. The days passed rather pleasantly, the nights full of hot passion that had been sadly missing. They loved going out to Kailas' for seafood dinners, cycling along the beaches, and generally making up for lost time that was speeding away again, bringing with it the dreaded departure of Nigel for Bundaberg.

The daily dropping in to Galliano's Café for coffee was something special. They were both habitual consumers of cappuccinos, with which they toasted each other on many happy occasions, none more so than the longed-for family that Tammy wanted to start as soon as possible.

When there were only two days left, they went to Gino's for the last time and found their favourite spot. The waiter came over, and Nigel told him to bring the usual. People knew the couple well enough that the waiter knew what "the usual" meant.

At a table near them sat a group of young men and women in board shorts and jeans, the girls with loosely flung sun-bleached golden hair. They languidly discussed what the typical younger Freo set usually sat and discussed over coffee. Around the corner came a freckled and emaciated youth who carried a large watermelon. Someone grabbed it away from him. They treated him with much amusement, throwing the watermelon from one to another whilst the owner protested vainly. Finally, they relented and gave it back to him, but only after he had promised to share the watermelon with them. He then whipped out a pocketknife and proceeded to cut it into equal shares. No sooner had they started eating their slices of watermelon than a waiter descended on the lot and ordered them off the premises, saying with authority, "You don't eat watermelon on Cappuccino Strip. Take the bloody thing somewhere else." This they did in boisterous fashion, with much laughter and hooting.

Nigel and Tammy thought the entire episode funny. Where else would you find such drama but in Fremantle?

When they got back, Tammy went to wash her hands whilst Nigel idly flicked through the day's *Australian*. He was softly humming a song. The clock ticked away softly on the wall. All these things pass away, it seemed to say. "Come what come may, time and the hour runs through the roughest day."

"Tammy, I want a divorce," he said casually, as if he were asking for a glass of water. The insouciance caught Tammy off guard. She came round the corner smilingly and sat down at his side.

With a laugh, she said, "Darling, you'll never guess what I thought you said. Sounded like you asked me for a divorce," she said with a little laugh as she played with a stray lock of his hair.

"No, you heard right, Tammy. This is the secret that I promised I would divulge later. Well, the time is now."

She drew away from him in utter amazement, breathless and stunned. Tears sprang into her eyes. "What? What brought this on? What cause have I given you that …?"

"No, Tammy, it's not you. It's me. I want a Russian wife. I'll be flying to Moscow in a month to get myself a wife. Sorry," he said, examining his fingers as if nothing else mattered.

"What happened to all the plans we had? What made you think all this up? It makes no sense, Nigel."

She left the room in tears. He could hear her sobbing. He went to the sideboard, got himself an apple, and began chewing it leisurely. Time ticked away on the sun wall clock sun that grinned malevolently at everything in the room. Half an hour later Tammy emerged, sunshades on. It seemed an appropriate way for a young woman to meet her personal tragedy. She walked past him, crossed the floor, and went out of the flat.

The door opened again shortly as she spoke from outside. "Leave the flat key under the door mat when you leave ... or do whatever you want with it. I won't be back," Tammy said. She was quite composed and conducted herself resolutely. She never went back.

What Nigel did thereafter will never be known. As any such ending should have, this had the iron of finality. For some reason, he wouldn't have been able to explain any of this. All he could think of after she had left was the memory of the acned youth and his watermelon on the Cappuccino Strip. It seemed funny at the time, but now the humour was lost on him.

Exquisite Chaos

When you taste a raindrop, you long for the ocean. You cannot drink the ocean because you were never meant to, so it leaves you with a thirst for it. You cannot look for heaven, whatever that may be, unless you are ready for it. That uncertainty principle partly explains some of the mystery of this existence.

Everyone, at some time or another, gets a glimpse of eternity. Sometimes wild grass gets in the way. At other times, it's a whiff of incense. Some claim they hear God speak to them, and that could mean trouble for everyone. I think I stepped out of time once. Maybe. Just maybe. I'm going to try to tell you about it.

Hey diddle diddle,
The cat and the fiddle,
The cow jumped over the moon.

Well, if the Eagle landed on the moon, a cow can jump over the moon, can't it? I don't care what the little dog did. Little dogs are dumb.

Plumes of radiation and chemical emissions had reached the highest heaven and had started to offend the delicate nostrils of angels who were busy trying to clean their contaminated feathers. Now they no longer joined in singing the "Hallelujah Chorus" without going all cracked and hoarse.

I sat drinking my Masters Chocolate Milk and idly contemplating the Shwedagon Pagoda that came floating past me, almost lost in clouds of its incense. You can't have any idea how I felt when I heard the voice of God asking me if I knew anything about his Mrs Mac's big pepper beef steak pie.

Me, Lord? I hope you won't be offended if I ate it, would you? I would have denied it immediately, but I was distracted by a hydrogen flow that kicked up a sort of tiny tornado that picked up Stonehenge and rolled it away, along with some weird white-clad crazies in drag who waved burning brands about whilst chanting something that sounded like a dirge. Who needed these weirdos in drag, anyway? All around the bluestone altar grew wild grass with guts enough to survive anything. Seriously wild stuff!

I turned to answer God that whoever had his Mrs Mac's big pepper beef steak pie, it wasn't me, but there was no one there. He had gone. I heard him coughing behind a cirrocumulus arrangement some way off. He was at it again, asking questions or complaining about something and then disappearing just as you were about to answer. No wonder churches had falling attendance as people left for Buddhist temples or Sufi training centres. Bishops had taken to selling pencils and "Eat one and get one free" Kentucky Fried vouchers to boost their thinning stipends.

Simon and Garfunkel and Paul Kelly numbers were being sung during pray-in sessions that had replaced masses. They skipped things like the Nicene Creed and rubbish like that these days of the Third Axial Spiritual Reformation. A lot of time had flown under the bridge, to use a cliché. Why not?

It was a couple of centuries later that I came upon a company of black Rwandan guerrilla fighters – or at least that was how they identified themselves to me at the time. There were five of them, all greenish black. With long-stretched necks and yellow flickering eyes, they looked like elegant giant Galápagos turtles. They were all armed with AK-47s. They had flattened the long grass and ferns on the coral-infested ocean floor that was now home to the boat that they had used as their pirate ship off Madagascar.

These warriors lay on their sides watching a crazy Arab with a bad dose of Parkinson's doing a wild dervish dance. It had turned out to be a bad mistake sending him out on a suicide bombing mission amongst the Antarctic fairy penguins. I briefly joined the Rwandans long enough to add my exhalations to the exquisite chaos and dream seeds into their already fetid pores.

God kept on grumbling "Leave them alone, can't you." He's forever hiding when he says things to me. I've told you that before, haven't I? It's such a bad habit, repeating myself. Bad for storytelling.

Suddenly, everything blurred. Kaleidoscopic colours swirled around me, splashing the most amazing reds, blues, golds, and purples. Planets and shooting stars raced away into what might have been distances, although neither time nor distances existed anymore, only improbabilities of the same. There was abruptly a void now.

I was propelled into another vision. I drew back in horror. That old and withered man was me. This must be the future. The land I found myself in was the Pilbara. I loved my life in that beautiful, hostile land. I was trekking again with people I hadn't yet seen and thus did not know.

"Serves you right."

There. Again. What did that mean, "serves me right"?

They were as old and slow moving as I was. One was a priest who wore black, and he was collecting a lot of Pilbara red. Another was a scientist collector of sorts who had a net and a bag of fossils. A warrior party of natives armed with long spears and nothing else accompanied us on our trek. They kept up a horrible droning incantation that none of them were enjoying very much because flies were flying in and out of their mouths. Those which weren't so lucky were swallowed without diminishing the number of flies that replaced them immediately.

I took time out and rested on a rocky outcrop, wiping my face. Perspiration ran in salty rivulets down my cheeks. Then everything changed forever. I was bitten by a gigantic white spider, and I cried out. As I went to kill the damned thing, the prospector who was really one of those research insect scientists that roam about with nets and backpacks full of VB, pushed me aside rudely and swooped on it with a jubilant cry, scooping it up in his net and putting it into his bag. He danced with joy whilst I died horribly in agony.

I had tried to protest my innocence, that it wasn't I, but to no avail. Before my eyes closed, I was aware of the warriors spearing my pain-wracked body. That white spider was their holy creature or a sort of god. Shows how much they need white anthropologists to show them what's sacred and what's not. But a white spider? Really! Twiggy Forrest has them on his payroll, or so they say. I want to know if a bloody white spider has ever bitten Twiggy. Dunno if it's true or not. Maybe not. Who knows?

Later my bones were collected from the desert and put into an empty forty-gallon drum that had belonged to a roadhouse dunny long ago. Father Murphy at the Mission, after he had dried out from his weekend binge, blessed and sanctified them. He sanctified bones when there were no kids around. They knew when to run for cover! I had come to be rather beatified. I didn't believe in all that stuff whilst alive, but at my death, ironically I was sanctified. That was OK by me. I felt that since I was dead, why not and what the hell! Now, that last word should not have been uttered. I could be held to account. There was no telling. But what the … heck (phew)! The desert must have been badly in need of holy bones, and Father Murphy was keen to give them those to please it, I suppose. I was never going to need them here.

"Holy bones, did I hear you say? Hee-hee-hee! More of the delusional stuff."

"These unholy dead are too much. Aw, stop it. Go find your own Mrs Mac's big pepper steak pie, you bully! Leave mine alone. Where's that St Peter? He's never around when you need him. Still showing pilgrims and tourists the finger from his throne in St Peter's, in Rome. Have you ever noticed that? All who've seen it think he's giving them a blessing. Ha-ha-ha! Can't seem to get him away from there."

Ho-hum. So much for myths and legends. They are meant to sort out what has become of our exquisite chaos.

Herriet Watt

Half the fun of going on a holiday is the beginning, calling into the offices of travel agents, getting as many brochures as possible, and chatting to travel consultants. It is all part of the happy and exciting planning. The imagination runs riot. One is suddenly keen to absorb the culture of the place, savour the cuisine in cafes and restaurants, feel like tourists looking to be entertained, and made to feel wanted if for no other reason than to let them extract as many of our travellers cheques as they could for their solicitude and friendly sharing.

We liked the style of Saga Tours, which had its head office in London. It was the only agency with the imagination to engage the universities to lease their student accommodation for the duration of the seasonal holidays when students were happy enough to go abroad themselves or simply to go home. It gave would-be travellers like me the chance to experience vicariously the tertiary atmosphere of our chosen universities. Besides, it was a lot cheaper.

We had let Saga Tours book us into what we were assured was going to be a great place to stay for the week we were in Edinburgh. We particularly wanted a taste of life in one of the halls of residence of some university, so our lot fell to Herriet Watt, just a ten-minute walk from Princess Street. Milly and I had always been curious about the lifestyle of university students in any university in the UK. I vicariously wanted to experience the ambience in a hall of residence. It fell to the lot of Herriet Watt or Durham in England to provide this satisfaction. In any case, it would prove less expensive than a stay in a hotel. So it was to Edinburgh that we travelled.

The early winter week proved very Scottish – grey with overcast skies and always blowing wildly, proving to be both forbidding and cold. Anyone who has visited Edinburgh knows how windy and freezing it can be down Princess Street. The total absence of sun and the endless biting winds zapped me psychologically. Looking back at the week in Scotland, I have to admit that the Herriet Watt episode in my life proved very memorable and humorous by way of an embarrassing incident. Humorous by way of hindsight only, I should add!

A broad buxom woman whose "broad" explanations I failed to understand – every word of them – showed us to our rooms. She reminded me of pictures I had seen of the forbidding appearance of Queen Victoria. I think she knew that she hadn't gotten across anything that she had said, but she chuckled after a fashion and went her way, still chuckling to herself. I wondered if any of it had been delivered in the Queen's English or the Scottish "English". I felt a lot of sympathy for the foreign students who came to live here for the length of their studies. I laughed quietly as I tried to picture a Pakistani or Bangladeshi trying to make out what the woman had just said. It would have been a lot of fun listening to the broad Scottish accent and the Bangladeshi or Pakistani accent in animated discussion. You wonder how they ever figured out what the other was saying. It must have been hilarious.

We learned a lot about the living conditions of the students who had to live here. We found that the beds were very hard and promised only spartan rest. The blankets were threadbare. Looking about us, we discovered that the hand basins were too small to wash anything in them; moreover, only cold water was available. The toilets were meant to be shared but rarely ever to be used by daft tourists like us. The toilet bowls were tiny. It wouldn't have taken a hell of a lot to fill them. You first had a problem squeezing into the seat and later getting up again if you were struggling with a weight problem. It certainly presaged a disaster if you allowed yourself to be caught short or contracted the runs.

I felt guilty bringing Milly into this set-up. I couldn't bear looking into her eyes, which had acquired the trapped look of an endangered animal. She gazed ruefully at the WC, I must say, but she refused to complain. Stout-hearted Milly! The only way to avoid using the toilets was to make sure we emptied ourselves in some hotel before night drove us into Herriet Hall. It wasn't a very welcome prospect. We prayed hard not to feel the urge to visit Mother Nature any time during the night, however agonizing it was. Even as I write this story, a cold sweat rises down my back.

The showers were located on the top floor. Access to them was by the use of the lift, which was the size of a shoebox, so narrow that two of us barely fitted in. OK, so maybe I exaggerate, but mind you, just a little; the rest I am prepared to swear to. There was worse to come. The towels we were expected to use wouldn't go around us fully. I'm tempted to call them oversized handkerchiefs. It was a mark of Scottish frugality, I supposed unkindly. This was a holiday we hadn't really wanted. It gave the impression that they catered for emaciated university students the width of matchsticks.

It fell to my lot to be the first to shower and to report truthfully to Milly what the experience entailed before she was prepared to attempt it. So I went in and handed over all my travel-soiled clothes to her. The plan was that she would bring me up a change of clothes while I showered.

I'm one who loves singing in the shower, but I swear screeching was more like it because the water was freezing cold and never warmed up. I took five long minutes before I decided I had had enough of the water torture for a lifetime and tried to towel up. It simply wasn't possible. Vast tracts of my body remained wet ... very wet. The nearly threadbare towel was suddenly saturated. This was sure to make poor Milly cry. And then came the worst of the disasters: there were no clothes to change into. Milly had forgotten to bring my changes. Or she had thought she would let me have a nice long hot shower. Ha! Oh dear God!

I cautiously peered out of the cubicle, praying to find her on her way, but no one was about. I listened intently. Still nothing. I was beginning to feel confident that everything would turn out OK because chances were I would not be intercepted on my way down in the elevator buck naked.

I had to make my way down the corridor, my derriere exposed to the entire world. The lifts seemed miles away.

Thank God we had the place to ourselves since the students were away on vacation. But not the domestic staff, all of whom were women. I heard some of them chattering away as they approached me, so I ran back to my torture chamber and quickly locked the door, shivering wildly, thoroughly wet, miserable, and now acutely embarrassed.

After they passed by, I ran the entire distance to the lift and went down to our room. I was a mere five metres away when I heard my tormentors on their way back. I could hammer at the door, but Milly could be at the other end, otherwise preoccupied, and it would take long enough to be caught in the raw by the not-so-wee Scottish lasses and what a hoot that would be ... for them. They had a flasher on the premises. I could end up arrested and charged! So I raced back to the lift, but the towel fell away in my haste. My modesty was now fully compromised, for there I was, naked as a jaybird, racing around madly. The lift groaned and jerked its way up, and I prayed to the Almighty to keep the women away from the shower recess. I had never before called so desperately on the Almighty for so many favours in my entire life. As I got in just in time, another couple of women came from the opposite way. It was a pincer movement to trap me. They giggled all the while, but if they found me as I was, they would have screamed with laughter and perhaps some lewd suggestions. They would have a story that would have won them popularity in the workplace, I'm sure. It wasn't every day that a streaker was found on the premises.

This running backwards and forwards could have kept up all day had Milly not discovered the towel when she opened the door and guessed what must have happened. She quickly relieved the situation by bringing me my change of clothes. She was so embarrassed. There we were, two Aussie tourists, both embarrassed beyond reason, but for different reasons. Whenever we recount our adventures in Scotland, this episode is sure to get a special mention.

Jesus of Napoleon Street

I had heard he was around here somewhere. I took it as the sort of whimsical throwaway line that comes up in the sort of dead end of inconsequential conversations that are punctuated by passing silences. People had last seen him in the David Jones lingerie section, taking a keen look at some Marie Clair stuff. You know, bras and shifts, low necklines … He scooped up a fistful of Baccis and gave them to a blonde seven-year-old girl who giggled at him. The huge Samoan security guy was down like a flash and frogmarched him away, probably saving him from the furious mother who kept screaming obscenities at him. He only smiled and advised her to love her enemies and those who sought to do her harm.

Lilly of the Fields and I dropped in for a coffee at Vann's and caught up with him. We really didn't know him at all, you know. Does anyone, really? Some people talked a lot about him. But that was only on Sundays, when he was nowhere to be seen. I'd seen him at Swanbourne Beach on Sunday sometimes. He was really cool on his boogie board. Some said he'd been trying hard to get back his skills of walking on the waves – but without any success. And as for the nudes of Swanbourne Beach, he's long since forgiven those who like to sunbake down there. That wasn't very hard to do.

Anyway, this day he was by himself in his usual brown hessian one-piece Middle Eastern sort of gown, hair matted, of course, and that stubble on his chin much too scraggly. Why he insisted on a mullet, I don't know, though Lilly of the Fields thought it was cool. He had a cappuccino in front of him as he went through the day's *Australian*, rather indifferently, I thought. A server was sent by an anxious manager to get him another cino, but he turned down all entreaties. They conspired as to how to get rid of him, I suspect, but couldn't quite work out a strategy. I thought that he could be short of cash. That's right, Lilly, isn't it? He was always on about not taking heed of what we should eat and wear. Poverty rather appeals to one who has made Centrelink lifestyle an art form. He recommended it to everyone, and many took him literally.

A group of four elderly women bowlers had filed through the door, all volubly discussing the day's games. They failed to notice Jesus's languid form at his table. They usually bought him a croissant and beseeched a blessing. The redhead, who had the shortest hair imaginable, tripped over his sandals that had been left in the way. She did a little jig and ended up in his lap. She was definitely more astounded than hurt and took ages to get up off it. Jesus smiled indulgently like some affable parent.

"Oops, sorry, Jesus."

"That's OK. Don't worry about it."

The fat one came back with a latte in her hand a few minutes later.

"And by the way, Jesus, what do you think of Julia[1]'s carbon tax, mate?" she said with a brown coffee stain around her mouth.

There was a chorus of "Yeah. What about that? No social justice."

Jesus held on to the redhead a little longer than was necessary and said, "Render unto Caesar the things that are Caesar's and unto God the things that are God's. The trouble with you people is that you don't go to church often enough or you'd have heard about it in the sermons," he said.

The old girls then settled down at their table, ordered lattes, and talked about Julia and the carbon tax in a most unhelpful way. Things were getting back to the usual uneventful sort of dull cafe stuff when a priest came bustling in and headed straight to the brown-robed Jesus, who had drawn his chair up to the table where the bowlers sat.

"Now look here, Jesus, or whoever you think you are, I'll come straight to the point. Stop calling me. I don't know how you got hold of my mobile number. I'll set the police after you for making a public nuisance of yourself," the priest threatened. He was red in the face and perspiring. "Anyway, what was it you wanted this time? Call the Parish Social Committee if it's another meal, not me. And stop asking for alms at the cathedral front door after mass. It's bad

---

[1]   Australian Prime Minister at the time of writing.

enough that the takings are falling without facing a growing competitive industry with you and your snivelling ways."

He sounded quite out of breath.

A rowdy group of young men burst in just then, sand in hair and sunburns in raw evidence everywhere on exposed forms. "Hi, Jesus. Giving Father a bad time again? Remember what happened the last time. You've got scars in the palms of your hands to prove it." They all laughed and sat down, calling for service. They were well known in the Cottesloe area as sand bums. They were all university students actually, but they seldom attended any lectures. They were certain to fail and drop out.

Father turned an outraged face at them but said nothing. He was too preoccupied with confronting Jesus, who gave the bowlers far more attention, which was a worry, especially the redhead, who squealed with laughter and thought his jokes were so cool.

"Can I buy you a coffee, Father?" Jesus asked.

"Never mind the coffee. What's so important that you dragged me down here?"

"He wants to convert to Christianity, Father. He was telling us all last week about it."

The bowlers all loudly backed her up. They drew up chairs and asked the thin, angular priest to join them. One of them even got up and brought him a cappuccino, which he reluctantly accepted, all the while staring at Jesus, unsure whether he should indulge the idiot any further. It would only make him bolder. They seemed to know each other fairly well, so there was no real problem … except sometimes when Jesus began teaching some awkward things, rubbish mainly but so infuriating. Father hadn't yet learnt to ignore Jesus of Napoleon Street and his stupid ways.

Some half an hour went by, and the lads were on the way out to their Jeep, where the surfboards were lashed to the roof. On his way out, one of them dropped a croissant before Jesus and mussed up his hair. They invited him down to the beach. Jesus picked up the offered croissant and took a bite. It tasted good.

One of them called out from the passenger side. "Hey, Jesus, why don't you try that walking on water trick again? You never can tell. It might just work for you just one more time. I'll get Seven's cameras lined up for the "Current Affairs" next week if you can pull it off. No sweat." They all laughed, and away they drove, gunning the engine noisily as they headed back to the waves.

Half an hour later, the women decided they'd all better get going. They had husbands to feed. Father went with them in a better frame of mind. He was easily pleased by the happy-go-lucky ladies and didn't mind a joke with them now and then. Jesus hadn't finished with him. Not yet. He stopped at the door and lit a weed.

"Bye, Father. And leave the little boys alone, you hear? You've got these fat tarts who love ya."

The fat tarts turned and gave him a beauty of a group raspberry. The redhead called out, "Wait till Herod gets hold of you, smart arse. You'll be sorry. Fancy a crown of thorns again, then, do yer? Some people ... you never know where you are with them. You must be into pain, you dumb shit."

"Bye, then. I love yer, too," called Jesus with a chuckle. He loved all of them, though they'd make lousy disciples.

Journey's End

It wouldn't be long now. For days, he had been thinking that way; it wouldn't be long. He had lost count of the times his nephew Jacob hadn't been expected to make it through another night. They had said it wouldn't be long now. They had been saying this for the last week or so, since he had heard the news about him and moved into the flat where his favourite, Jacob, had lived alone these past twenty years. He and Jacob were the last of the Barusch family of the Ashkenazi tribe who were from Poland. Jacob shouldn't have to die alone. Where were the rest of his family? Bertha had died many years before, but he had six sons who now lived all over the place and out of touch, unlike good Ashkenazis. It was impossible to get in touch with them. Was it a matter of choice that they stayed away? Had they become so dysfunctional? Yahweh had forsaken this sad family.

On trembling and arthritic legs, the ancient uncle groped his way through the dingy room with misty eyes, in a silent sort of ritual, peering at the bric-a-brac that accumulates around one through life, each one a little milestone in one's life journey. In the life of a European Jew who had lived in the previous century, such a journey wasn't a happy one.

There in the dining room, in a sacred cabinet of their family tabernacle, lovingly wrapped in faded and ancient linen, the old man found a battered old copy of the Torah. It had been allowed to accumulate so much dust that it began to look grey. In a quavering voice, he softly sang the Schema as he picked it up and blew as much dust off it as he could.

It brought tears to his fading eyes. Inside it were lovingly scrawled the names of Jacob's sons. Jacob would have acted out the role of patriarch as he read from it at his family gatherings. His voice would have grown weaker with age over the years. The circle of listeners would have gradually lost their rapt and devoted solemn attention to the warm drone of his voice. Then they would have begun disappearing. The long road of Jacob's tormented life had become littered with failures. How sad it was to go over the many failures.

He could hear the doctor moving about the room. Perhaps he would bring some good tidings after all. Perhaps there might be some small reason for hope. Hope was all there was left to cling to. The doctor came into the room on his way to his car with hardly a glance at anything else, ignoring the old man, and then he was back again with another black bag. He gave the same scant attention to the anxious uncle who was left with unasked questions in his ancient eyes that were bleary with the fatigue of the years.

The old man found a sweaty old yarmulke on a shelf near the picture of a younger Bertha, who smiled through the lost years. The photograph looked like a daguerreotype that had been cherished and loved. It belonged to a time when it had been easy to smile. Jacob had been such a proud and holy man who walked like a god with family to the synagogue in full view of the community in those years. They were a highly respected family.

The years of the holocaust visited the old man; they were rarely far from his consciousness. The surviving Jews had seen it coming, and those who had the money and courage pulled up roots and fled to all parts of the world, wherever they could, to whoever would accept them. Tens of thousands of Jews fled Europe; millions filed their way into the ovens to be exterminated. The Barusch Ashkenazi found their way to Israel, which was the land of their dreams and hopes. They would restore their fallen fortunes, and all would be prosperous again. Justice would attend their endeavours for the rest of their lives.

Soon, however, Bertha died in a blast a suicide bomber set off in Tel Aviv one happy sunny October day outside a market. Death had followed them to the Holy Land. Over the years in Israel, they didn't know a day without violence. They learnt to be hard and hate their Arab neighbours. Hate was the currency that bought them survival. The sons had all been soldiers who were taught to kill, and they were heard telling of their longing to kill as many of the bastards as they could. They would talk about what they planned to do to the prisoners they took. Jacob knew it was time to move again. And soon. He was losing his sons to war, and he watched and heard them surrender their humanity, their most precious gifts of life, to hate and violence. Whilst there was still a modicum of it left, they had to be rescued, so he brought them all to Australia. Australia was proving a land of promise to all who had been displaced after the war, a land of promise to all who had fled persecution and terror, a land that promised them all a bright new future.

On a small table by the side of the old sofa was a photograph of Saul, with his long flaxen hair and enigmatic smile. There seemed to be so much promise here. So much had been expected of him, so little delivered. One day there had come a knock on the front door – there were two burly Australian police officers informing Jacob that his son was in detention. He had become involved with the sale and distribution of amphetamines. Nobody heard from him again. Saul, oh, Saul, what have you done? You were to be our messiah. What had happened? Years later, Jacob received a brief letter of apology in an unsteady scrawled hand. Then it was that Jacob began the sad and slow descent into depression. He never really recovered.

But where were photographs of the other sons? What had become of the others? The old man sighed and sadly shook his frail head.

The old patriarch harboured these thoughts in his heart as he became lost in memories of the past and the present crisis of the family, culminating soon in the dying of his nephew, his beloved Jacob. He didn't hear the doctor leave, so he couldn't have heard him say, "He doesn't need me anymore. Call a rabbi and an undertaker."

Standing outside the closed door, he intoned the Schema repeatedly.

Lampshades and Cushion Covers

Eric Hausmann was brought to Australia by his grandson, Gustav, on a tourist passport last year. He had been diagnosed with a rare form of blood cancer. The doctors at Cologne Medical Centre were the best in the country in the treatment of blood cancer. They knew that an eighty-five-year-old cancer patient didn't have long. They advised him to enjoy what was left of his life. His granddaughter, Griselda, had been writing almost every week, begging him to come to Australia for a farewell visit. The old millionaire had a special spot in his heart for her. When she decided to settle in Australia and later married Dr Peter Portelli in Perth, it broke his heart. The doctor was a prominent oncologist and would be qualified to help the old man.

Old Hausmann decided he would go to her even if it meant his death. He persuaded Gustav to get him there. He was strong enough at present but would soon be incapacitated. It was a race against time. It was a race that Eric Hausmann won when he reached Australia at last. Griselda and her husband, Dr Portelli, met Gustav and Eric Hausmann at the airport. With all the usual airport formalities behind them, at last they sped away in Peter's BMW to Dalkeith, where he and Griselda had their palatial home.

Hausmann settled in and enjoyed being in Australia. He found the indigenous people a never-ending source of curiosity. He would have liked to have spoken to one or two, but he was openly contemptuous of them, just as he was of the number of Asian people he found in the shopping centres. That is why he began withdrawing from going to the shopping centres, which he saw were institutionalized – that is, places for commerce as well as offering social centres for people to mix and enjoy their days and evenings. This was offensive to him.

And so it was that when he was taken to the Rhine Danau Club in Melville, he was overjoyed. Here was a place of refuge, a haven where only people of German extract were welcome, it was claimed, although he discovered from time to time that non-Germanic people came and passed time occasionally. He resented it and queried the necessity of tolerating this from those he had come to know recently, but he found himself being patronized and even humoured. He'd always hated that. He eventually cut himself off from most of them.

He also found himself isolated and ignored. At times, he thought he caught some of them looking oddly at him but quickly averting their gazes when he stared them down. When either his daughter or his son-in-law picked him up later in the evening, he tried to draw that person into some discussion about his growing isolation, but the driver always changed the subject, showing no interest.

Dr Hausmann would come into the Rhine Danau Club every morning at about ten, order his first Heineken, and take it to a darkened corner of the reading room, where a cluster of pot plants cut him off from the usual clients, who by then had come to respect his desire for anonymity and seclusion. He browsed through some old German magazines scattered about on the tables. He sipped his beer whilst staring out at the world and ruminating on any bit of news from Europe. Occasionally, someone would come and take his empty glass, asking if he would like another, to which he usually nodded without looking up. The beer would arrive, and then he would mechanically pay and retreat into a world of his own.

The Rhine Danau ran a number of interesting functions. There was the table tennis that could be played anytime there were challenges afoot. Some preferred the endless rounds of darts that went on nearest to the bar. Every now and then, cheers arose as some proof of great marksmanship became evident. At one far end, there was a special corner for the TAB, for those who liked a flutter. A race would be viewed in eager silence, but soon a stream of profanities followed as the favourite was beaten, or when a wager proved successful, there would follow a call for drinks all round.

The Rhine Danau was "Ossified" German in culture, which meant that it was German without the politics, although that would be passionately discussed by the oldest Germans who had come out of a war-ravaged Europe. Memories never dimmed, but the patrons mostly managed to get rid of the vitriolic language of the Nazi dialectic. Where once hung photos of contemporary right-wing diehards now hung photographs of famous German soccer players.

For the literati, a separate room functioned as a club library and contained the German classics and contemporary

philosophers and novelists. All the books were in excellent
condition, which might suggest that they were not patronized
all that frequently, thereby signifying the successful
process of "Ossification" that was ineffably underway. And
through all this sat the morose, lonely figure of the wealthy
Hausmann. Time swirled past him in its entire delusional
ambience. The past never really deserted him. There were
things he never let go, sadly enough.

On a stormy day in June one year, the door of the Rhine
Danau swung open to admit a tall silver-haired man wearing
an overcoat. Despite his greying hair, he exuded a boyish
charm and inner health that could be referred to as radiance.
The club manager, Roger Goltz, came out of his office and
greeted him in a friendly manner as they shook hands. He
invited the newcomer into his office with a shout over his
shoulder to the barman. "Hans, two coffees, please. Make
them strong and hot. That's the only way Dr Eleazar and I
drink it. Right, Doctor? Come on in and tell me about your
visit to Berlin. How do you like the new Germany?" Soon
the voices died away as the door closed. With this, the two
were soon ensconced in the luxuriously appointed office of
the manager of the Rhine Danau.

Closing time drifted into the club, which usually had very
few left inside before that. The lonely figure by the palms
remained unmoved. On this occasion, a long shadow fell
across his body. Nothing was said. The newcomer looked at
the seated figure. The seated figure sat slumped, waiting for
his daughter. He looked at his watch once or twice.

"Hello, Herr Hausmann. I am Dr Eleazar. We haven't met.
I have only this last week returned from Berlin," he said

politely. He was ignored, which made for an awkward few moments. In the distance, the anxious figure of the manager could be seen hovering uncertainly.

Eleazar sat down without Hausmann asking him to. He perched at the edge of the chair. Briefly, he recounted his assessment of the new Germany and its multicultural composition. His voice echoed the cautious optimism of the new Germany that was unfolding.

"What do you miss most, sir, of the old Germany you knew and what you would like to revive?" asked Mr Eleazar.

The old silence returned, but with a certain hostility. A fly buzzed past a plant and banged into the glass plate that cut off the outside world of the club. A car pulled up outside. Hausmann's daughter had arrived. The car door slammed and the clicking of her high heels could be heard.

"What did you say your name was?" asked Hausmann, without so much as looking up for a moment as he asked the question.

Almost eagerly, the good doctor repeated his name with a welcoming smile.

"Eleazar. David Eleazar. Dr Eleazar," he replied. "I was asking about what you missed most about the old Germany you knew, sir."

The old man arose uncertainly on his feet. He advanced the two feet towards the doctor and looked him up and down through two steely blue-clouded eyes.

"Lampshades and cushion covers, Eleazar. You people made such damned fine lamp shades and cushion covers in Auschwitz and Belsen," he replied with a cackle. He drew himself up to his fullest, stared Eleazar in the face, and then brushed past him on his way out with a smile.

Lazarus Today

The silence of pain and darkness was all that reality came to mean to me. To survive the visiting spasms of insanity, I had to believe that was all I could expect. There were often bright flashes that I associated with lightning. This was really the passing of the years. There were the sudden claps of thunder that burst upon me even when the skies were unclouded, but more so when dark clouds turned day into night and then night went on forever and ever. There would come the sounds I hated most of all and which sent pain waves crashing through my head: the sound of chains and the opening of the metallic door. Then there was that other sound – the sound of my screaming. The sound of her screaming…

In my hell, time had ceased to exist. I felt that I had become insane, probably incurably insane, but then I told myself that if I could still think that, I couldn't be insane. Maybe even if I could think I was insane, I was indeed still insane.

Then everything abruptly changed. For what reason it all changed, I cannot say. It is still quite beyond me. I often heard myself screaming when I was first led to experience sunlight; it brought flashing headaches. For months, I wore glasses all the time I was outside.

Visitors dropped in from time to time to see me. Some dressed in white and had what I gradually realized were clipboards in which they made entries. When a woman reached out to me slowly, I flinched and found myself cowering as if to protect my head. I adopted the foetal position for protection.

My surrogate "mother", which was what she had repeatedly asked me to call her, quickly but softly took my hand in hers. I had come to welcome her touch and ministrations, and they drew me away. I found myself in her embrace and her tears wet my cheeks. There were no more men with bull-hide whips and metal torture implements. I was given food regularly. The food was always tasty and the fruits so sweet. Life became very different, and I lived in a growing fear that it would just as inexplicably be taken away one day. This must be paradise.

I found that I could go out whenever I wanted. I frequently wanted to go outdoors, where beautiful birds flew down and spent time around me, sometimes looking for food and sometimes merely hopping from branch to branch. It all seemed so foreign to me at first. I was always aware of the lovely woman I came to see as my mother cautiously watching me from a distance.

One day a strange propulsion took me to her. She watched me anxiously at first. A slow smile chased away her creases of anxiety and uncertainty. She took a couple of steps in my direction. I immediately stopped. Something wanted me to flee; something made me hold my ground. I felt the sound welling up inside me. I felt it make its way up into my throat. An energy inside my mind threw the sound out as my hands rose to greet her:

"Mother!"

I heard the cry. It was incredible the load that suddenly fell away from me. Sobs wracked both our bodies for some time. She gently pulled away as she stared up into my face. That vision expunged the horrors that once were my only reality. I felt that vision would help me build myself again.

They came again, the white-coated people, and we went out to meet them. They pulled up shortly in their four-wheel drive. They clearly didn't know what to say. A look of sheer incredulity was plastered on their faces. When they went to step out, one of them held the others back with a sharply whispered command.

I couldn't allow them to stand there forever, so I pulled away from Mother and approached them with my arms extended. I found it nearly impossible to find language for the occasion, but they didn't. They were profuse and exulting. I heard mother softly tell them it would be time before I would regain the use of words. We all needed to be patient.

I walked past the group to the four -wheel drive and rubbed my hand over the chassis. I was stunned by the splendour.

The leader came up behind me. He opened the door, looked at me gently, and said, "I tell you what. Why don't we all get in and go for a drive?" He helped Mother and me in, and the rest of them piled in. The engine roared into life. I felt the energy of the powerful engine flow through me. It was wonderful. We were off and speeding away into the desert. I saw the world flashing past – shrubs, dunes, trees, and always the friendly smiling blue sky. This was how reality had become for me. Life was flashing past before my eyes, and all I felt was a torrent of a happy energy that lifted me out of myself and made me a part of the newly emerging reality.

We returned after about half an hour. I heard the leader spit out an imprecation, and he braked sharply. I heard a sob from my mother. I looked out and my blood ran cold. The world had darkened, though there wasn't a cloud in the sky. There in front of us were two half-tracks. Outside, a group of armed men were facing us. Worse, I recognized all of them, especially the one I called the devil.

I don't know what happened next, but I awoke in pitch darkness to the sound of chains being dragged across the floor. I saw no people, but I could smell them. Where was Mother? I felt betrayed. The feeling was worse than any physical torture and suffering at the hands of these monsters. I sat up, listening hard for the voice to pierce my mortality calling me. I heard only the sound of coarse laughter and the crying of what I realized was my mother's lament. I heard her calling out to me, but I couldn't do anything. When you are called into life, you enter a world into which you may have been born but all has changed. The world is no longer the same, nor is Mother, nor the people who lived in that world and in that time which was another time.

I heard the sounds of another life. I don't know why I sat listening for the call again that would return me to the world in which I wouldn't be a refugee, for you can't find refuge in any other world and time except for the one in which you were once before you died. There your mother grieved, would have grieved, over your death, but in dying you left her in her grief. Now you still hear her lamentations and would hasten to comfort her except the voice no longer calls to you from beyond. The one who then called me out was dead. They had killed him. History – or is it narrative – says he died on a cross. I wondered if he, now called Redeemer, was the same one they kept calling into what they call life in all the churches all over the world and if he also had to and has to come out also plucking all those horrible worms from his half-eaten body. I know how upsetting that can be.

Life Is an Option

The winter of 2009 was one no one was ever likely to forget. Storms had rolled in from the west, accompanied by thunder and lightning. The rain had fallen in frightening torrents that transformed the Swan into a raging nightmare. The water flowed close to the overhead bridge in swirls and eddies. It bore the detritus from the suburbs that lined its banks with branches that storms had torn away from trees. This made any crossing extremely hazardous.

Traffic over the Fremantle Bridge had fallen away noticeably as accidents led to a frightening number of fatalities.

An unexpected lull in the storms had brought a few intrepid but curious watchers whose self-imposed reclusive lives had become tired of the winter. An angst had spread like a contagion that had been noticed by doctors and psychologists as the visits mounted steadily, as had suicides. There had already been three such unfortunate deaths. Reporting on this malaise had made the media complicit with the burgeoning problem, but a story is a story after all. It's fair game for media moguls to sell more papers and draw more TV watchers to the next six o'clock episode.

People appear to be fascinated by such reports; an aspect of personality actually feeds on what scares the hell out of one. I personally think it offers viewers a feeling of congratulations that they themselves are still in the land of the living. They would survive come what may, even if the feeling threatened to wilt as the winter dragged on.

The sun that had remained hidden behind black leaden clouds all day managed to find a chink where a crack had unexpectedly split the cloud banks for a while. The bridge was almost deserted. On the ledge near a supporting column where adventurous people hoping to catch some fish for the night meal would perch on stools brought for the long haul. The prospects had died down; no one was that game now. This made the figure sitting at the edge of one nearest the bank a figure of some mystery and fear for his safety. If anyone felt the intimation of a coming tragedy, it failed to do no more than raise a distant curiosity. The figure of a man was lost in total immobility. It was not known how long he had been sitting there, nor what the purpose was.

Suddenly, there were two. Unaccountably, another had joined the man, but from the shape and mass, it had to be a boy, which made the sight more compelling, but as of yet, no one had decided to intervene to protect both of them.

They learned later that the boy was eight years old. He had drawn a large black plastic bag around himself. The two occupied the gloomy perch as they stared down at the black raging water below. Only once did the man look sideways at the stranger who had decided to join him. But he ignored him.

"It's getting cold, isn't it? Soon it will be raining again, I suppose," the boy ventured, but the man ignored him. Silence was legal tender in a siege such as this. The boy seemed to know this. He had made a few attempts earlier. As long as the old man said nothing, he was safe; there was no chink in his armour against the world. No one could get through. It didn't stop the boy from keeping up the well-timed chatter. It wasn't anything immediately one after the other. There were weren't any pleasantries or inane topics that would come easily to some eight-year-olds – nothing about footy, nothing about cruel fathers or dumb mothers who never seemed to understand their children.

It went on like this for some time. Light on the bridge had come on. Lights in homes along the riverfront were coming on. The boy stuck it out. A strange camaraderie had settled in. Now the older figure turned and addressed him. It was no more than just the odd word or two, sometimes something longer. Now he shook his head at times; now he stretched an arm to point to something across the waters to the opposite bank.

Unknown to them, a small group had begun gathering some distance away. A taxi had disgorged its occupants. A ute had stopped by. From its interior cabin, a match briefly flared and smoke shot out into the deepening gloom. The driver called out to the nearest person, asking what the f*** everyone was staring at in the dark. Two or three made a move to investigate, but a woman in a rather thin plastic raincoat held them back. From under the head of the raincoat, tousled wet and scrawly hair poked out. It was strange that she had chosen to interfere with an attempted intervention when anyone else would have urged it on. A few stood back, looked at her, and asked her why she was stopping a rescue, stopping people from doing something.

"But I am doing something. As a matter of fact, I am ensuring that the man's life will be saved," she said.

Someone let out a coarse, derisive laugh and said, "And just who the hell do you think you are and what the hell do you think you're doing? Try stopping me. I'm going in to take the boy off the ledge."

"No. Don't move towards the pylon. The man may jump." There was a note of authority in her voice.

A woman at her elbow spun her around by a shoulder and asked, "Who the hell are you to take charge when you won't do anything useful yourself, you bitch," she ground out.

"I'm the boy's mother," she said matter-of-factly.

The identification stunned everyone. Some drew sharp breaths. Others asked no one in particular, "What the hell? The mother?"

"Let me tell you all something that you need to remember all your lives. Life is an option. It is something my son, as young as he may be, has always lived and acted by. I saw all this a long time ago and came down because I was afraid that you would break the resonance that had been established between my son and the desperate man on the bridge. It would lead to the man jumping into the river. In a minute, he would have drowned. He had no desire to live. He had to be shown that life is an option. He had to see it, feel it for himself. Whatever the burden he carried that had drawn him to suicide was unimportant. Only life mattered. The boy has always known this and has taught his own parents this invaluable lesson. His name is Elijah."

By this time, the two bedraggled figures from the bridge had made their way up to the gathering. The old one momentarily paused and put his hand on the boy's head and smiled, but he didn't say a thing. The sound of a police car's klaxon sounded briefly. Red and blue lights swirled as two police constables came out to see what had taken place. Clearly, someone had phoned them to investigate the growing mystery. They took the boy and old man aside and briefly spoke to them, and then they put the clipboard away and shook hands with them. They went on their way, visibly relieved.

Before the old man left, he pulled off his cape and revealed himself for the first time. His hair was as tousled as the boy's was. He said something unintelligible. There was a whisper in the crowd, which had grown a bit.

"He's Chinese," someone said.

The old man stopped and turned around. He said, "A human being, actually."

The drama clearly over, the crowd began dissolving, realizing the day's entertainment had concluded. Now it was back to the other dramas, but all on TV this time.

The mother, with her arm around her son, headed for the road where their car had been parked. They spoke to each other in the soft and gentle language of love. No undue excitement, no admonishments, no extravagant praise. It was just a mother gathering her son to herself with a quiet pride and special understanding. After all, his name was Elijah.

McFaddan's Cat

Ole McFaddan had a cat.
Ee-i-ee-i-o!

No, I'm not going to sing the whole song today. It gets a bit rude in places. My wife and I came across this mysterious animal only after we had bought a house in Linden, a small rural town, population about two hundred, a few miles south of Margaret River, off the main Busselton Road, and had barely been a month settling in.

Our neighbours, whilst being helpful, weren't exactly friendly. You know what it's like – being helpful but not friendly. We can be a bit like that ourselves. Well now, just a bit about the cat that you should know something about. It was supposed to answer to the name of Blanche but rarely did. I find that most cats are like that about answering to names or terms of endearment. Arrogant they are, introverts and sly, unlike most dogs, which are more extroverts and love human company. They are known to eat anything offered to them. Not always, I don't suppose.

But to get back to Blanche ... Blanche was a beautiful white moggy. It had red eyes. That threw us when we first came across it on our front doorstep one winter morning when it was so foggy and wet. That was when the wife, Betty, saw it. She, being the first to see it, came darting in and breathlessly made the announcement. "I want you to come and see this white cat. It has meandered into our house. It has red eyes."

My first reaction was to scoff at this. Red eyes! Huh! Betty had a way of seeing things. Then I saw it myself. White and vertical, its tail was slowly wagging, and soundlessly it called to us, after which it licked a paw and then looked around. Yes, the white cat had red eyes. I looked at the eyes many times to confirm to myself that indeed they were red. I had heard of albino cats, but I knew that they were very rare. Nearly each one was said to have mysterious powers. I wondered why it had come into the house. I wondered if it was hungry, so I asked Betty to give it a saucer of milk. The cat looked at the milk, yawned, turned its back, and then wandered out. Betty locked the door, and we left it at that.

It was winter, so we rugged up and went up the road some distance away, where there was a small shopping centre. Australians don't have marketplaces but shopping centres. On our way there, we met the portly Mrs Brady on her gopher. She overflowed it, actually. In the short time we had been residents in Linden, Mrs Brady had come to know us better than most others who we were happy to call neighbours. She was full of anecdotes about not only Linden but also the district itself, which also included Margaret River. She considered herself an amateur historian. Her histories included a lot of gossipy stuff about everybody too.

We'd reached the town centre, happy for her company, when the white cat passed us and went across the road. Mrs

Brady choked off what might have been a gasp and crossed herself. She hissed quietly, "It's that cat." We said we had been visited that morning.

Mrs Brady went white and said, "I feel I must warn you about that animal." The warnings were dire, but I won't go into all her details.

The butcher also revered the white cat. He never failed to leave a saucer of milk out for her – or even diced pieces of fish, which Blanche obliged by devouring. We bought half a dozen lamb cutlets and went on to get some fruit and veggies. I bought a book about wartime exploits of Aussie diggers in Vietnam. Linden was just the place to spend time getting in some reading.

And so our earliest ninety days passed in this sleepy hollow of a rural community. One afternoon we were sitting around entertaining Jack and Jackie Smith, whom we had come to cultivate as friendly neighbours, when there was a knock on the door. Once I opened the front door, looking somewhat like a breathless anorexic, Mrs Oberman came in wild-eyed and in some distress.

"Jack, get home quickly. Is Jackie home or with you?" She didn't know Jackie was there too. She was in the kitchen with Betty, discussing the intricacies of a Chinese chicken soufflé.

"Oh, there you are, dear girl, Jackie. Thank God. I felt you should know that I have just seen Blanche sitting on the roof of your house. God knows how long it's been there." After apologizing if she had upset anyone, Mrs Oberman mounted her bicycle and rode off with a tinkle of her bell. What followed came as a surprise.

A strange hollow-eyed look came into the eyes of Jackie and Jack as each looked at each other with some thinly veiled trepidation. They excused themselves shortly and left after some rather forced light-hearted comments about silly cats.

We didn't give it another thought, but shortly after the New Year arrived, we got the news that Jackie Smith had returned from hospital after being diagnosed with breast cancer. This sort of news usually is very unsettling to friends, relatives, and those who know the victim, and so it was with us. We dropped across to see them. Jackie seemed quite composed – the usual sort of Jackie we had come to know. We'd decided to keep off the commiserating a bit, until she or Jack told us what had befallen her. We had a few beers, and after an hour or so moved to the door as we took leave of them. Betty had stayed back for a minute. Jack looked at me. "It's that bloody cat," was all he said.

The incongruity sprang to mind to force a mild sort of critical retort, but I left it unsaid. It might be his only way of dealing with the initial shock of the terrible situation they would now have to face. How many others had died without Blanche having anything to do with it?

However, word in Linton got around. Some even suggested shooting the bloody cat. Maybe old man MacFaddan should be asked to leave town, taking the bloody animal with him. He was one of the oldest living residents of Linton, having seen off some hundreds of predecessors. God only knew from where he had found the white cat or even if the white cat had claimed him in some strange way. No one wondered why he hadn't been the one who had been the first to die off. If he wouldn't leave town, then they should ostracize him and put pressure on him so he lived a thoroughly miserable existence, leaving him no choice but to leave.

Jackie died some nine months later. Linton was in mourning. The little Lutheran church three kilometres out of town buried her in its adjacent plot, not that the Smiths were Lutherans. They didn't attend any church, but Jackie and Merlene Schmidt, the vicar's wife, had met and a friendship had followed. The Lutheran minister, Aage Schmidt, agreed to bury her. At the funeral service, some sombre twenty or so village people attended to give Jack support. He was half out of his mind, poor man.

A short distance away, a white cat viewed the entire proceedings dispassionately. Its tail swished slowly from side to side. It yawned and then with unhurried insouciance strolled away into some shrubbery and was lost to view.

Back home, getting dinner ready at the end of the sad day, I switched on the TV to see Judge Judy settle some ridiculous cases as usual. It interrupted the solemnity of the present real life. It was a fortunate escape from life, even if only temporarily. Halfway through the show, Betty poked her head around the kitchen corner and in a querulous manner asked, "I don't suppose there's anything to it?"

"To what, darling?" I replied, dreading the answer.

"What's being said about that damnable cat," Betty said.

I tried to laugh it off. "There's a huge cat mythology that has spanned many diverse cultures around the world, dear. It all started in the Egyptian imperial age, some five thousand years ago, when the cat was venerated and deified. Who knows how that happened or why? Isis took the form of a white cat when he called a human soul off to the afterlife. The cat itself was said to have nine lives. Cats are said to have nine lives to this day, not that anyone has bothered to actually count them. In China and India, the cat is a minor deity and worshipped too. People are taken in by the drama of death that is touched by the coincidence when our deaths are somehow linked to sightings of cats. It doesn't have to be a white cat. Some see the black cat as being even more malignant, a cat to dread. Every person has a similar story to tell. Why the story got such a hold on people is hard, if not impossible, to tell, but it has. After life here in Linton, I imagine you too will be able to enhance its potency in the next town we may shift to, with an even more elaborate mythology, I dare say. No, love, it's all whatever one may want to make of it, really. No more. Come and watch *Judge Judy*. This is a whole lot more fun, thank God. It's an escape from all this."

Try as we might, as time passed, we found we couldn't hack it in Linton, so we called up the only real estate rep in town and put the house on the market. Betty had succumbed to the subtleties of the cat myths, and she would probably enlarge them, sadly. I didn't mind leaving. Linton hadn't really grown on either of us, so it was an easy decision to leave when the time came. We had bought a unit in Melbourne and moved all our things there.

On the last day, we looked about the house we were leaving one more time to make sure we weren't leaving anything behind. We weren't leaving anything because we had carefully packed up everything, but we weren't leaving traces of the red-eyed white cat behind. When we were seated in the Holden and strapping ourselves in, Betty had some trouble getting the buckle to hand, and that's when I saw it.

Right in front of the car, I saw Blanche cross the road. It stopped and eyed me directly, then floated away. My knuckles whitened as my hands gripped the wheel more tightly, and I drew a deep breath.

"There, at last I got it!" said a relieved Betty as she clicked the restraint successfully and stroked my hand on the wheel with a smile.

I tried to make light of it and sang in lively falsetto:

> *Ole McFaddan had a cat.*
> *Ee-i-ee-i-o!*
> *Ole McFaddan shot the cat.*
> *Ee-i-ee-i-o!*
> *Is anyone surprised by that!*
> *Ee-i-ee-i-o!*

McFadden's cat is a story dedicated to the army of witches and those with predilections for spiritual bent who see things no one else does. As you might gather, cats are not my favourite animal. Give me dogs anytime. More people have died unheralded by the previous surreptitious appearance of cats, be they black, white, spotted, or brindle. Cats do offer exciting conversation topics and story time openings for stories like "MacFaddan's Cat", with or without the "Ole MacFaddan Had a Cat" ditty.

Return to Haworth

It suddenly occurred to me what I had to do. The night settled down rapidly after all that emotional turmoil. I opened the door and inhaled the fragrance of the rose garden and my mystery made palpable. Oh, the magic of it all. Those who don't believe in magic need read no further.

As long as this power remained, I would paint this night with the magic of it all. Even as a child, I would often paint, the stable floor my canvas, the horses stamping in their own steam – always very long-suffering with the wild boy in the urine-warm atmosphere of the stable. They would have seen convoluted figures dripping on the floor.

All this she knew all along – now long since dead. That and the disportments of hell I splashed with a brush dipped in lime. Now a headstone in the Haworth cemetery behind the sad little church was all that remained, that and the crying in the night of a love that would not die. She knew I looked for pain, but only she knew why.

Secretly, I think I feared the rose garden. I had always feared the locked gate, whose latch awaited the merest touch. The desolation of the dog roses, the cracking sides of the forever-empty swimming pool seared by the rainless summers of recent years, sounds of laughter and splashing when the pool was full to overflowing in happier days …

There was so much activity around the mottled sundial that had been sold nearly half a dozen times – flitting from shadow to shadow. Tonight everything was bathed dully in the silver light of distant Cassiopeia.

There. I heard it again. A voice called to me from the darkened room where crumpled bed sheets trailed across the bedroom floor.

But my thoughts went out to another far away, the person to whom I had to return what I had already given her: awareness. In me was her meaning. She needed to possess more clearly the awareness of this meaning.

How close the stars were. Ancient. Pristine. I wondered why she had given me so much of herself. It had been too much of a burden to carry these two hundred years. Should I go to her now, I think I would know all. She had spared me nothing as I had wildly danced in the blood lanes of her fevered mind that echoed the moanings of the lost winds of the moors.

My name drifted out to me again. Heathcliff. Heathcliff. Querulously. Passion has an insistence that feeds upon itself. It becomes a burden. She would have me back to wring from my body her last. ("Roses are red, violets are blue," she would sing in her tuneless way, eyes half-closed, her face framed in swirling cigarette smoke.) The mind can be a fearful emotional junk heap, but I was not unduly perturbed. I had learnt to find contentment from loneliness. Moors and loneliness are too strong to deny. Their massive brooding was always in my soul.

I have friends who are very vulnerable; they curse their clay. Empty whistlings of down winds echo in the interstices of their sub-dermal caverns. I had often been there. I knew. I knew I was dreaded. She, too, in Haworth, had known and had flinched. I had to know tonight, and I too flinched and trembled. This was madness, I kept telling myself, crying softly in the night.

My hand rested gently on cold iron. The latch clicked open. I was engulfed in the rose garden. The low-lying hills silhouetted in the distance seemed to warn me of something. Why? Here was peace, or what passed for peace.

I heard nothing, but my blood pulsed in answers to questions I had yet to ask. ("Nothing is, my love, as sweet as you.") The crazy song followed me around from room to room. From a very young age, I had always had a love/dread of silver-shafting starlight. Millions of years lay spilled around.

She stood in the doorway. A cigarette glowed. She was beautiful, nude out there in the moonlight. "Kathy, go back in. We'll speak in the morning."

I wondered why I had said that when I could have just as easily spoken about what we had to talk about to release each other from our torment. I could not understand why I had chosen to defer it to another time.

Kathy was always all the lonelier in one of her cold rages, like tonight, a beleaguered nymph. It clothed all she was to say. She spoke in a low voice. I wondered if I could later recall all she said just then. I wondered if I would ever be able to return from Haworth, where the one with whom I was indeed obsessed had lain since 1849.

"Listen, Kathy. It's there."

"What is?"

"I don't quite know, but it's there. In Haworth. I have to go."

"You must be out of your mind! Haworth? What's got into you?"

"What I've been striving after. Straining every fibre in my body. That's what has got into me."

The words came out in a torrent. The night came alive with sounds. It was a world of discordant chords in which I seemed to make out the cry of a helpless victim in the claws of some nocturnal bird of prey. Rustling in the rhododendrons. Fluttering in the pine tops. The air set in a maelstrom of unknown passions.

Her small white breasts flattened against me. I clasped a body that had been suddenly drained of its passion. It was like standing on the shore of a lake listening to the retreating ripples of waves. I had known those waves before this, when they hadn't been quite so gentle. I well knew the tumult of which the waves were capable. They had hurled me to where the sky had come down and left me breathless.

I was not unaware of how much I needed Kathy. Those whose destinies are forever fused together know this need. It is what sets everything in motion from the start, a motion neither of the two understand or control. Kathy knew this and didn't care. I, too, did. I was determined to find out more about it. There seemed to be something outside of me that expressed this terrible desperation, this obsession that wasn't quite so magnificent but before which one could become vulnerable.

"Why? Why?"

I realized how tightly my fists had become clenched, so I slowly opened them.

"What's that?"

"Sillion and star shine."

I gathered her up in my arms, my poor little victim. I didn't need an altar stone. I felt her fear coursing along her veins. I then set her down gently and let my hands rest lightly on her buttocks.

"Sillion and star shine? What are you on about? Sillion and star shine? You're in another world, Heathcliff. You're weird. What's got into you?"

"We have to return what she gave us, what she put into us, Kathy, she from whom we were born."

"She? She gave nothing she didn't want for herself but failed to find. We are the ones having to pay."

"Are you sure?"

"Yes. You are mine, and I am you."

"I understand what you mean, Kathy. I know why you must love me, and the answer is to be found in us as much as it belongs to her own mystery. Tonight I must a way and find out once and for all why I had to be for her what she wanted for me as much as for herself. It's never let me rest, just as it gave her no peace at all."

I had nothing more to say. I was empty. Silences can prove fatal. There's a letting go, an instant release. After that, there can be no recovery. Such a silence settled in there. What happened next is irrelevant.

The night exploded in a flood of invective, and in the torment of sound, I heard the clang of the gate behind me swinging shut. It sounded so final. Down the way that none dared to walk, I now turned my footsteps. And then – I know that I shouldn't have, but I did – I looked back.

Like a wraith swathed in a halo of incandescence, she had thrown her head upwards towards the night sky. I turned away to hide from that wild piercing cry that rolled in pitiful echoes from moor to moor: "Heathcliff, damn you!"

Balladonia

Vikko had been happy working as a bouncer at the Oasis nightclub somewhere in Perth. I don't know where exactly. I don't know Vikko, for that matter, but Jose did. I can't recall just how he talked me into getting Vikko out of Perth as quick as possible because there had been an altercation with someone who turned out to be a member of the Devil's Angels, and you didn't mess with them and expect to live. It wasn't my quarrel, so I shouldn't have had anything to do with it, I told myself, but somehow I was quite helpless. Vikko could be quite forceful in his persuasion, as I well knew from previous incidents. So here we were in my beat-up 1960-something VW, which was groaning and coughing as we made our way out of Western Australia, keeping a watch for black-jacketed motorcyclists bearing down on us.

Cyclone Vance had sputtered out a few days ago. Passing through Widgiemooltha, we drove through the last lashings of its waning fury. The sky was still grey and the roads still waterlogged in places.

"The police released the name of the man towing six wheelie bins behind his gopher on the Kwinana Highway. He had been singing lewd songs and—"

I turned off the radio. Vikko and Jose remonstrated. They laughed like hell at the thought of the idiot who must surely have been drunk. Why did regional radio carry crazy stories like that? I wondered. To make dreary country lives bearable, I supposed. Humour was a great relief from boredom.

The scrubland looked a sorry sight, more greyish than green. It had just missed the rains that had flooded the country farther north. From the top of a slag pile which had become a lookout point, we had seen the inland sea that Vance had formed. The usual salt pans had all become one large inland sea. The grey slag heap on which we stood had rivulets running down its steep slopes. It had formed incrementally over the years from the gold mine for which Norseman had become famous. The sky was a darker grey and threatening. A strong wind ruffled the bushes and skinny trees along the way. An afforestation attempt was being made to return trees where the miners had cut them down to feed their boilers for the production of gold. The saplings rose like an army of spears, young and slender. It would take a few decades to be fully grown in all their majesty.

A combi van had pulled up off the highway, and an old couple were enjoying a cup of tea or coffee. He was bald as an egg. She had her hair in curlers. What was that for? I wondered. That alone was a very odd sight. They waved slowly. Waving enthusiastically expended too much energy, and that was in short supply at their stage in life. Jose called back something – I'm not sure what, for it was lost in the wind. He was an inveterate caller out of inanities. I had this problem with him. Maybe it was just as well the poor old dears couldn't have heard him after all.

And then there was Balladonia before us in all its splendour. If you've been to Balladonia, you must think I have an eccentric sense of humour. It looked sad and stranded like a forgotten attempt to arrest the emptiness of the outback, but all it did was emphasize the immensity of the undertaking. It looked a derelict gesture – just a weather-beaten and sun-baked cafe and its service station as well as what passed for a motel that had long since ceased taking itself seriously. An ancient rusty boiler struggled to stand up as a proud but sad symbol of something civilization had thrown out in despair. The shingle reading BALLADONIA ROADHOUSE was sandblasted and fading in a patchy sort of way. Who'd care in this godforsaken hole? There it stood remorselessly devoured by salt and sun.

Three twenty-wheeled juggernauts were drawn up whilst the crew enjoyed the meagre hospitality of denim-ed, bearded, and rather scruffy angels of the lonely travellers. We ambled up to the bar and ordered a round of the amber "oh-be-joyfuls", aka Carlton Mid-strength. It went down beautifully. The stuff slakes thirsts and invigorates life. The exhausted drivers were not inclined for conversation, as Vikko and Jose soon found out. After a couple of rounds, we hit the dusty red world again. There was a ways to go yet. Vikko had someone meeting him at Cocklebiddy. There my good turn would end. Hopefully. Jose was financing the getaway, but the enigmatic Vikko would have met some of the expenses. Not that I had done anything to deserve it. So? What the hell! I was waking up to the fact that I was a victim of circumstances and my slow thinking.

Fate intervened in the form of half a dozen motorcyclists who roared in from the west. They were the Hell's Angels from whom we had fled. All hell would break loose now, I feared. Vikko and Jose, who must have been the first to see them, were the first to move. They had returned to the combi and were slumped down low inside. I tried to crab across to the van as casually as I could, not wanting to show fear or guilt or draw any attention to myself.

They had clearly questioned the barman, and they came out into the sunlight, put their helmets back on, and pulled down their sun visors, looking even more sinister. They stood for only a few seconds checking out the combi before beginning a slow and maddeningly frightening steady tread to the van. I had a sudden urge to urinate and wondered at my chances at being extended the courteous gesture of availing of the comfort before dying. Jose had clearly decided he would pretend to be asleep, and he began a fear-fuelled snoring that could have fooled no one. In better circumstances, it might have even been funny, but here and now, no one was in the mood to laugh. Certainly not the Hell's Angels, who wrenched open the combi van door so violently that they all but took the side off.

"Gee, lookie who we have here! None other than our old mate Vikko. Anyone would think he was trying to hide from us," said the one with a large flying moustache.

"Not nice. Not at all friendly, I say," snarled the one with the Viking helmet that had two cow horns protruding from the head plate.

"Naw, not at all, so we don't need to be friends with him, then. The boss would like a word with you, sunshine," said the third brute, who had a strong squint in the right eye and the smell of an overflowing cesspool.

They might not have known it then, but they were going to have a problem: three motorcycles and four who needed to travel. We weren't waiting to see how the problem was going to be solved. Jose urged me to get as much speed out of the combi as possible. There was a good friend, if Vikko ever needed one. I did not waste any time debating the ethics of the highways and byways as I crouched over the steering wheel and almost stood upon the accelerator, but with hardly any difference to the speed we got out of the groaning machine.

I didn't think Vikko was a great long-distance runner, and I sure as hell hated to think there was a shovel tied to one of the Hell's Angels machines. I didn't notice any, but then again, I had no reason just then to think such thoughts. We'd find out soon enough. I didn't think their boss really expected to meet with Vikko at any time in the future. Nor did we.

Cocklebiddy

It was hot. Dancing waves shimmered in the distance, and the haze was filled with broken images of the timeless land, brown and red and dotted with thousands of grey-green wilting bush that was all the vegetation the country was able to support. The Eyre Highway rose and fell like a black ribbon over the undulating surface until it straightened itself out and lay like a tired snake of mythic proportions, stretched out and exhausted as it ran fading into the distance.

Scotty was driving over to Adelaide in his early vintage model Holden to try to bring Debbie back to Coolbellup. There had been a falling out during a drunken session in their rental ramshackle unit. When Scotty came to his senses some months later, he decided that he had some serious issues to sort out. Debbie had to get back into his life. He knew where she'd be holed out in Adelaide. He hoped she would still be there, although she hadn't bothered to answer his calls.

You could never be sure what you'd come across once you were out on the Nullabor. He'd driven trucks over there a couple of times when he drove for New Farmers Association, and he'd seen some remarkable sights, but nothing prepared him for what came his way some ten kilometres before he hit Cocklebiddy.

The beauty of the wide spaces of the bush often present you with spectacles for which you are totally unprepared. These are sometimes charming and exhilarating, sometimes macabre, sometimes exotic. Sometimes you think you must be hallucinating. Bushies take it all in their stride and say nothing of it, but the townsfolk have to stop sometimes, rub their eyes, and stare.

As far back as he could remember, a red uncovered dirt track had been running parallel to the Eyre Highway after cropping up from nowhere. Now and again, these ghost trails had a way of cropping up, leaving people wondering who had made them, when, and why. Usually you'd see dust devils, tumbleweed, or desert briar come bowling along until the wind that drove them had died. As far as he knew, nothing else ever used the red dust road trails these days. Until this day. And then he saw something that made him wonder whether he should laugh aloud or make the sign of the cross solemnly. Or perhaps both.

An ancient black hearse drove along the red dirt track, churning up a cloud of red dust in its wake. It was driven by a hair-gelled blond driver, a callow youth of sorts, who peered out of the windshield from behind thick-lensed spectacles. The red dust on the windscreen didn't help much. It followed in the wake of an undertaker who looked properly dressed in black from head to toe, black top hat and all. He mopped his face with a large red handkerchief from time to time. Scotty knew he'd be drenched in perspiration under his undertaker's dress. He thought the man had to be seriously mad. And that went for the idiot behind the wheel. In the hearse was the coffin, covered with gum tree branches and what once had been purple desert rosemary and lavender flowers.

Scotty pulled over to the side a few metres ahead and waited for them to draw abreast, and then he got out of his car and rested against it. He pulled out a half-smoked cigarette and lit it. This couldn't be for real. Who in the hell was in the coffin, if anyone at all?

"What youse got there, matey?" he called out.

The undertaker ignored the question. He must have heard him, though, unless he was deaf as well as daft. Looking straight ahead as before, he proceeded with the greatest dignity. Only the lad behind the wheel of the hearse looked sideways; he then swallowed and tore his eyes back to the front, gritting his teeth. And so they proceeded to what surely must be a cemetery of sorts somewhere nearby.

"Where yerrz gonna dump the poor sod?" asked Scotty.

His earnest question was also treated with disdain. So he shouted the question again but again was ignored.

"See yerz, you dumb bastard! Make sure you bury him deep or the dingoes will get him," farewelled Scotty after offering this piece of unsolicited advice. They again ignored him. The youth behind the wheel glanced out at him a couple of more times but quickly looked in front as if he may hit something. He didn't seem very confident behind the wheel. He was probably off some farming property where kids were known to begin driving in the paddock without adult supervision.

He got back into the car and drove alongside the hearse a while longer, until his thirst reminded him that Cocklebiddy was not all that far off. He gunned the engine and tore off down the Highway with a wild whooping. Later, when he looked back to see where the hearse was, it was nowhere in sight. He wondered where it had detoured. There hadn't been any dirt tracks turning off the main red dirt road, if you could call it a road.

If you haven't been to Cocklebiddy, it's just a place on the map. It is concealed from the rest of the civilized world, which is unaware of its obscurity, and that goes for many Australians as well. Cocklebiddy probably cherishes its concealment from the rest of the world. All around it are treeless expanses of shrubs and truly nullus aborum, which means "no trees." There were shades of brown, red, ochre, and a tinge of greyish-green where shrubs and bushes eked out a precarious existence. Now and then, a few grey-green eucalyptuses promised some shelter, and you might occasionally find a handful of tired cows sitting in the mottled shade.

Into this hell of a desert, some poor dearly departed body was going to be deposited. Scotty was never able to discover just where. He went back and forth to meet up with the funeral party, but the hearse had disappeared from the face of the earth.

The scrawny, sweaty tawny-haired bloke with a sad squint who ran the pub in Cocklebiddy grinned knowingly. He wasn't going to fall for that trick. He'd heard stories like that before – like Spacelab falling out of the sky somewhere in the outback. Scotty dusted himself down and was glad to buy a middy of VB, which he downed in a flash. The barman smiled, shook his head at the story he was given, and poured Scotty another on the house for sheer audacity and inventiveness. Scotty was glad enough to down the amber life-giver, and then he went outside slowly, his eyes peering closely into every likely spot. He finally gave up, starting to worry about his beginning to see things. Anyway, it was time to move on. The succession of ridges ahead of him waited patiently. Twenty-wheeler trucks bearing the legends of various multinational and national companies ran up and down the highway. Scotty wondered if any of those drivers might have come across the cortege, and if so, what they would have done.

Mundrabilla

A goanna lumbered across the Eyre Highway and disappeared into the surrounding scrub. In a land where time was intended to stand still, it knew all the secrets of survival … as long as it didn't lumber across the intruding black asphalt ribbon where demons from another world raced madly to meet deadlines. They had all but wiped out the indigenous fauna in the desert land where now no vultures fly. Judging from the white crosses dotting the never-ending stretches of the highway, it would seem they were trying to wipe themselves from the face of the earth as well.

This was no place for human habitation, let alone any civilized existence. That is why there were only fifteen remaining residents there today; their destinies lay in the success of the commercial venture that was the roadhouse which provided a comfort stop, petrol, diesel, spare tyres, and food and drink for the itinerants who raced about to fill the shopping centres with food and other products associated with civilized existence. The roadhouse community would never get rich, and they knew it. They had no illusions about their fate. That is not why they choose to live there. Their roots, they claim, go all the way back to the sheep people, to the Afghan cameleers and the nomadic aborigines who now seldom make an appearance. History has claimed its own.

Life was made exciting by the small wildlife park they served, featuring a trio of scruffy emus and four iconic camels who spent their time dreaming of their past glory, or so it seemed from the way they slept off time that had changed things so enormously that there was no room for them beyond the wire fence. This they could not understand. Kangaroos hopped about lethargically when it was feed time or when there was some disputed issues to settle. The aviary brought the community the only sweet sounds from the desert. Mundrabilla was not altogether without some tenuous claim to fame. Fragments of a meteorite fell many years ago, more than any living soul can recall, and now lay scattered over an area sixty kilometres km wide. It was said to be one of the largest remains of meteorites in the world. The heavens had taken an interest in this remote part of the great Australian wilderness when there was no one living here. This, too, was part of Mundrabilla's ancient history that few could claim.

I'd fly a tiny Cessna into Mundrabilla whenever I felt like a break from the stress of Adelaide corporate life. I'd make a couple of stops along the way to get there. Some time ago, Craig, who owned the Mundrabilla Roadhouse, his son, and two locals had cleared away a landing strip and erected a wind-socket of sorts to help me. They did a good job of maintaining it, for which they were amply rewarded. It was all I needed to get in and out. I was the talk of the social circle of our law firm – Anderson, McGregor, and Luciani – and my colleagues made no secret of their chatter about their elderly eccentric senior partner. They'd often asked me what takes me out there. They were amiably confused.

I laughed them off. They would never really understand. I had been coming here for about four years now. I discovered these outback desert places – Balladonia, Cocklebiddy, and Mundrabilla, to name a few of them – when I first drove over with my family about ten years ago. I then promised myself I would return whenever I felt the urge to visit them, and I have been doing so ever since. My wife no longer accompanies me on these trips, ill health preventing her from doing so, but she never stopped asking me about my visits. The desert, I knew, had also claimed her imagination as it did mine over all these years.

The desert exerted a rugged and powerful spell over me. A primordial energy flowed all around me, enveloping me in its mystery. I admit that I could not claim it is a common human experience. I rather doubt it, but somehow I tend to believe that maybe it does even if one doesn't care to admit to it for one reason or another. The experience could be below the level of consciousness, but it must be there all the same. That could be one reason that most human beings feared it and would rather move away as soon as possible to feel safe. For them, deserts are not friendly places. For others, they were a source of rich contemplation, inspiration, and strength.

In Australia, civilization dared to encroach upon it from time to time: roadhouses; petrol, tyres, and batteries; Coca-Cola and beer; cheap accommodation in lumpy beds; twenty-wheelers and tourist coaches; detritus strung out along the black ribbon of a highway, including empty beer cans and bottles … Then there was LIZ WUZ HERE, obviously the work of some graffiti vandal.

From on top of the Hampton Tableland, a desert wind bears down in winter and chills the marrow, and in summer it burns the skin and cracks it open. Looking out from a vantage point, one is acutely aware of the insignificance of man. It made me wonder about the exaggerated sense of our importance in the scheme of things in the universe. A quietening experience, it humbled and restored one's sense of proportion, giving one a clearer picture of our place in the cosmic scale of life.

Everywhere we look, as far as one can see and far beyond it, there was once an inland sea where waters roared and teemed with life. When it all drained away, it was forever, leaving behind it a dry and thirsty land that gasped for life. This was a red world, prehistorically alive, that now had to tolerate the intrusions of this tawdry civilized world from the coastal fringes of Australia, which were now teeming with what Stephen Hawkins once called "chemical scum floating on the surface of the world." His views were scarcely complimentary. I was aware of another view, a view of the waters draining away and leaving the imaginations of struggling life forms dreaming their dreams of life coming into being and passing away in the enfolding eco-drama of the millenniums. An urgency about the aesthetics of this endlessness summons the tribute of the senses.

I loved places like Mundrabilla. For me, they put things in true perspective. There looms a religion that predates the ones the churches and temples think they own, with their man-made creeds and empty rituals that are meaningless to me. I believe the Bible shares this perception. It speaks of Jesus often going away alone into the desert to pray and to gain insights. I believe that he was never quite happy with what was being said about the reality of which he was aware. That reality is much too immense to talk about but still hammers away at the deepest levels of one's consciousness.

Send for Eliab

Overhead, vultures explored the air currents that were cooler than the burning earth below. If they looked down on the brown earth, they would have seen very little life. The earth was a hostile and rocky place of little promise, which that had once been cursed by an evil god. Vultures rarely descended in a search for life.

In the middle of what once looked to be a pasture stood a broken-down red tractor. It stood stranded in scorched tall grass and weeds. It listed to one side. This was the scene that the traveller examined from afar as he wiped the perspiration from his brow. He stood gazing in the pain of recognition. Despite the neglect and desecration of time, nothing much had changed. He recognized it nevertheless, though he had been gone these last twenty or so years. In all that time, no word had reached him about the history of those years. As a much younger man, he had ridden on the tractor as he went about his work during harvest time. He remembered the times it had broken down and he and Dathan had scavenged parts and repaired the tractor. It couldn't go on like that. He had begged the old man many times to get a new tractor, but his pleas were ignored. They could have afforded it, but

Dathan wouldn't support his demands. Dathan was the elder son and the favourite.

Eventually, Eliab lost interest in farming. The hardened earth had hardened the core of human life. He shook the earth off his hands. He undertook other duties but was always asked to do something else he didn't care for. Whatever he did wasn't good enough. Dathan rarely spoke two words to him before the sunset on any one day. His father coughed, spat, and brushed past him when he happened to be in his way. There was usually a muttered curse about something. Painful memories came flooding back. This was his old homeland. The earth, the trees, and the rocks made him feel he was home. A curse from hell had brought him into this family.

Eliab spat into the dust bowl from the side of his mouth. He descended the slight declivity and rounded the shoulder of a slight outcrop of rock that held pockets of earth, home to scrawny weeds and a basking lizard that scuttled away as Eliab came round the shoulder. His feet shifted slightly in some loose earth, and rubble ran away from under his feet, which fought for balance.

Before him stood the old family home, now a tired-looking mass of timber and a corrugated iron roof. A wind blew through the broken windowpanes. The front door was ajar. It seemed that someone might have accidentally left it open – or deliberately, as if it was certain that there was no further use for the house. There was no coming back, nothing to come back to. It was sad to reflect on the life to which it now stood witness. Ghostly echoes of children's laughter in play seemed to linger. Every now and then, a woman's voice was heard calling, calling, followed by excited shouts from children at play. He thought he recognized his own voice calling for Mother. The dancing afternoon dust devils carried the voices away in successive phantom cries.

An emaciated dog stared sadly and vacuously through eyes that lacked light in them; they were merely lustreless orbs. It lifted itself with a great effort and slunk away with a limp into the interior to escape, if it could, the flies that now even tormented Eliab. Its ribcage protruded miserably, poor thing. He wondered where it came from and whose it was. They had never had a dog that he could remember.

The wind flapped his damp shirt around his perspiration-saturated back. He turned when again he seemed to hear that woman's voice. It was the voice of his mother. He still couldn't decipher what she was calling out. The words swirled too quickly into the darkened interior. He loved his mother the most and leaving her was not easy. She haunted his thoughts into depression until time ate away the hard edge of the sadness and left only a persistent sense of guilt and depression that he could not shrug away.

Eliab cautiously entered the house. Curtains hung like ghosts in tatters and danced around in macabre fashion every time the wind blew through the empty house. The sofa was still there, the stuffing half out. Everything was coated with thick dust that flew up as he passed his hands over it. Nearby stood two upholstered chairs that also had all the signs of tragic abandonment, now home to dust and spiders. He walked around the lounge, each footfall sounding muted on the dust-laden carpet. He approached the escritoire which stood against the wall. The faded Degas print looked sadly back from above it. There had been happier times, it seemed to say. He stood looking at the tabletop wistfully. This was where the old man conducted his business and determined the family fortunes. Eliab wondered what had led to this show of destitution, the calamity spread before him. The enormous emptiness of his old home brought a sob from his parched throat. Unsuccessfully he searched for a secret history. He searched for a clue to the tragedy. Life had disintegrated rapidly, it seemed. Why?

Again the anguished cry as a tumbleweed came dancing in when another gust swept past him. Through a broken window, he saw it as it came to a halt in the distant corner to join a collection of former detritus. This time it carried the bass mutter of the old man's dissatisfaction about some domestic detail. He heard girls cry out, demanding something or another, as the girls were wont to. Eliab smiled sadly. Many memories struggled to register in his feverish mind.

He wondered where Miriam had gone. She would be married by now. There would be children. He wondered who her husband was, how they could have met, and where they might have met. There was no trace of her. He had got on well with her, especially the day after he found her out in the bush somewhere. She had fallen from her horse and hurt her ankle. He had carried her home. She became very close to him and supported him against the wiles and bullying behaviour of Dathan. He had tried to keep his brother out of his thoughts all this time. He was one reason he had to leave home and seek his own fortune far away in the big cities. There was no love lost between them. Nothing ever went right for the brothers. One reason was that the father loved Dathan more and didn't mind showing it. For Dathan, there were only smiles; for him, Eliab, there were only scowls and a show of annoyance. And his mother pretended she never noticed all this. When he had complained, she shook her head and told him to run away and play and not to imagine things like that. It filled his heart with sorrow and anger.

In the end, all this proved beneficial because one day he left and went far away to make a life for himself, where he believed he could be happy. He didn't have to wait too long. Things looked up for him. Things did go his way. He soon got work, digging ditches at first, and then he worked in the fields for farmers. There was no shortage of menial work. Having no special skills, he knew no other way of working. In time to come, after living frugally, he had saved a small fortune and bought a small farming property. He had built a solid future as a farmer in a distant valley where he met and married the orphaned Sarah. They had no offspring yet. He doubted that they ever could. He suspected that their time to have children might have already passed. For both of them, a pang of sorrow always accompanied the thought.

His past never left him. Days and months would pass without it stirring in his deep consciousness, and he would shrug it off. Then he would hear his mother. Then he would hear his sisters laughing. Then he felt he would like to get a glimpse of home because home it still sadly was. It held him in thrall. It was like the stirrings of a guilty thing. The devil's grasping hands tore at his mind. When the news came, it came unbidden. He had met a stranger at an inn. They had had a few drinks and got talking, and eventually Eliab realized that the story he was getting was really about the property that lay like a ghost, without any tenants or owners. The description was a clear enough indication. Through sly questioning, Eliab learnt of its fate, of what had befallen the family. Some details of the stranger's story were garbled and weird, but that was the way of all gossip.

All this passed through his mind as he wandered about the echoing house, where invading currents of air stirred sounds from distant times. At times, he had to stop and listen to try to catch the words. The library was full of cobwebs. He'd rarely visited this area of the house. There had never been a reason to. Books meant nothing to him. His father never shared it with anyone.

His hand reached down to the right-hand drawer. It mildly protested with a whine, being disturbed after all these years. He rummaged about. None of the accumulated papers meant anything now. A manila envelope caught his interest for some idle reason. So he opened it and withdrew a folded sheet of paper. He felt he was intruding and that he shouldn't be doing this. He sat down in a puff of dust and began reading.

As he read, a picture slowly came to mind. It was a letter to his brother, who, after all these past years, had come to live an estranged life from the family for some unknown reason. There was no evidence about any sort of rift or enmity that had come to separate them. It was all so strange. When he looked more closely at the letter, he saw that it had in fact been a letter that Dathan had returned to his father without comment. It wasn't a very lengthy letter, but what hammered Eliab's heart was what must have been the last request of his aging father to his favourite son, a request that had been earnestly made to Dathan, a request couched in urgent tones. The only words that burned in Eliab's mind were "Send for Eliab." That was all. "Send for Eliab."

The words jabbed him with a sadness that he had never experienced before. Now that it had hit him, it hit him forcefully. He gasped and sat down. Dathan could not bring himself to reply to the impassioned request for assistance. His father had admitted to needing him. His father.

It was a dying man's last request that the favourite son had felt unobliged to fulfil. He crumpled the paper in his fist, withdrew a box of matches, burnt it, and watched it crinkle into black carbon waste which curled up, now red-rimmed as the flame died out. He wanted to hate that brother, but a stronger emotion washed over him. His heart broke as he recalled getting word from a stranger who had spent days looking for him to carry the news of the death of his parents, first his father and then his mother soon after, for she refused to live a day as a widow.

He wondered why he had bothered to return to the empty house when there was nothing he could do. There was no one to meet and no one to greet him. He wondered if Sarah had heard the news and if she had come secretly and buried his parents but was too frightened to tell him, hoping that he wouldn't find out. There was a chance that he wouldn't. A new flood of a strange emotion filled his heart as he thought of Sarah. He recognized the feeling as love.

He looked around the house slowly and hoped they hadn't died alone. Dying should always be a farewell of love. He heard a noise and looked up. The lean and starving dog stood at the door, its head drooping. Only half of the dog was visible. It was too afraid to come any farther.

The Shadow Life

Carlos Jesus Morales lived in a ramshackle jarrah frame house at the end of the street, which led out into the bush a couple of kilometres out of Margaret River. No one there had any idea how he came to live in Margaret River or when he first got there. They came to accept the man from his occasional intrusions into the township when he needed to do some shopping. From time to time, he got work labouring in some vineyard or doing a stint with some road gang. He knew as much English as some sixth-generation Italians or Croatians who somehow never bothered to get a good enough education to speak the language properly, but he was always able to get by somehow. He lived by himself, paid his rent, and had no friends. He never bothered anyone, and no one ever bothered him. This was one reason Centrelink never showed any interest or concerns about him. It was as if he never existed.

I was the only one who might have gotten anywhere knowing him, although "knowing" isn't the word I want. I had taken a break from doing my research towards a PhD in the paranormal. My friend Bluey Watson, who played double bass in The Living Dead for a precarious living, moved to Margaret River for the duration of his band's contractual three months in summer, and he asked me if I'd like to go with them just for the hell of it. I had no hesitation and moved into a rammed earth cottage with him and the three other members of the band.

We did a gig every afternoon in the Timberlands pub on Main Street. This day was no different. I had my feet up on the railing and was having a Budweiser to relax me. As I sat staring in front of me at nothing in particular, I thought I saw someone or something pass across the drive into some shrubbery alongside. I didn't give it another thought. Could have been anything. I got up and went inside, where the gang were having a few rounds of poker.

"Deal you in, Bo?" asked Krassner, who played the saxophone.

I declined and said I was going up the drive for a stroll and might drift off to the town centre that was about five kilometres farther. I swung my jacket over my shoulder and put on my fedora.

"Don't lose too much, you guys. Make it no more than a buck limit," I called over my shoulder.

I couldn't play poker when I was sorting out some thoughts – wouldn't have been able to concentrate. I strolled along enjoying the air, which was slightly cooler than it had been yesterday. My rambling brought me to the little church, which was now in ruins. They told me it had been built the year Margaret River was getting built. It was now the rendezvous of lovers, discarded condoms saying so, and someone still shooting up, as needles said so. They were still there in the open, although they said the place had been cleaned up.

I went over and cleaned up a place at the base of a church window beneath which had been spray painted some grotesque drug-driven horrible painting of what was meant to be dragons coiled in combat. I then sat down, stretched my legs, and lit up a weed.

After a while, when I became restless and decided to move on to town, a shadow passed over the wall, moving in my direction. It didn't just switch off but rather dissolved into the brickwork. If it hadn't been for the previous experience not so long ago, I might have shrugged it off. I asked myself if I was hallucinating or if it was some other problem acting below the level of consciousness and surfacing for some reason only now and then. It hadn't done so before. Margaret River was the beginning of my shadow life, and I was still undergoing it.

I had lost track of time, and now the afternoon had passed and it was getting dark and colder. While I was starting to get up, I heard movement from inside the ruins of the church. I turned to look, fearing an attack from some louts, but it was only Carlos Jesus Morales, the harmless old man, and he tried smiling at me. He looked stranger than I'd seen him look this strange before. I nodded and said hi. He came and sat down near me.

"Hello," he reciprocated. He asked me to sit a little longer. I thought I should. It would be a rude rejection of his overture if I got up and went away. Somehow I felt myself wanting to stay and know this reclusive figure. Warily I sat down, nodded, and said OK, but very cautiously, not knowing what was going to happen next.

He took the twig he had been nibbling out of his mouth. "You saw it didn't ya, boss?" he asked with a little cackle that was meant to be a laugh.

"Saw what?" I asked.

He shook his head admonishingly. "You know. On the side of the old church a little while ago."

I didn't say anything for a while, and then it came to me that I couldn't bluff this old shaman, if he was that, any longer. He seemed to see through my denial. It unnerved me at first.

"Before that, you saw the shadow on the drive too."

He seemed to have a strange power. Anyone who knew all such things must be empowered in some strange sort of way. I grew still again. This was all very new and I needed to find a way of dealing with it. I found my pulse had quickened, as had my breathing.

"Only you could have. From the time the band started playing and from when I first heard you sing, I knew I had to meet you. You are shadow man," he said.

I had no idea what he meant by "shadow man", but I swear I was wishing I weren't. I wasn't cut out for this sort of baloney.

What was I doing sitting and listening to this yellow-toothed man? He wasn't just a stranger. Most of the folks here could be classified as that. Me to them and them to me. No. He was a strange stranger.

He played intently with a little spotted ladybird insect on his extended hand, laughing and saying something to it.

"You don't have to fear the shadow world, Bo. Is it OK if I call you what I heard the others call you? Bo?"

I didn't know what to say or how to accept it, so I swallowed and nodded my consent. What else could I have done? Inside me, something kept wanting him to stay and talk some more. I, strangely enough, wanted to find out more about him and what this shadow life was really all about. One thing was certain. I was never going to tell the others about it. I'd never live it down.

"There is two of everything. Two of everyone also. This world may not be the real world, but it's the only world. Do you know this? Of course you don't. But you are closer to it than your friends are. They wouldn't have seen the shadows that passed you. It was a black dog that roams the streets and forest. It does not interfere with any animal or person. It is the part of the shadow life that is in you that allows you to see what no one else can. It is in your music, Bo. Music is your spirit. Music is the noise that the others play, the sounds they make on instruments. Very pleasing but has no soul to it. You are different. I knew it from the moment I saw you get off the tourist coach."

The meeting was clearly near the end. Carlos Jesus Morales stood up and made to go but paused and said," Before I go, let me just warn you, my friend. Not all shadow world beings are good. Some are evil. Your death, whenever it comes, will be from an evil one, and I have no ways of knowing more than that. Your world will be the shadow world from where you first came and to where you will return. The future is always hidden from all eyes."

He promptly left, as if he had already said too much. He left me in a sweat of fear and incredulity. I didn't know what it was I had experienced. But my world has never been the same. I didn't ask to know all this.

Some years had passed since then. I completed my PhD and lectured briefly on the paranormal at college. I'd given up the band. I played very seldom and only at home. My wife and I were years older.

A long time ago – how swiftly time passes – we had a beautiful black Labrador named Prince. He was so handsome and regal in appearance and so soft-eyed and so full of life and love. We adored him and used to play with him for hours. He proved to be a very intelligent dog. He was incredible. Every day at four o'clock, he would come sit by me and nudge me. He wanted dinner. I would pretend not to notice, so he would sit closer and nudge me again. If I pretended not to notice the hint, he would crash through his doggie door and bring in his dinner plate well battered by years of use. I would then say "OK, Prince. You know where the food is kept. Go pick your tin. He'd run into the pantry and with his nose slam the sliding door open and pick out a tin, bearing it in his mouth until he dropped it at my feet. Then I would open the tin and give him his meal. I could go on and on telling you about his other achievements, but space and time denies this. So I'll end this by saying that eventually, after fourteen years and some months, suddenly Prince died. It would take too long to give you all the sad details, so I'll just go on.

We had him cremated. The point I am labouring is that he still lived at this address. Many a time, a shadow or something like one would pass. Either Milly or I would notice it, and we both concurred. We both experienced this strangeness that filled our lives with a warmth and sadness every time it happened. It wasn't a daily occurrence. Occasionally, I might be reading at the back when I'd hear his plate scrape the floor. The plate was made of light aluminium. How could it have moved? Did a breath of wind move it? We never ignored such visits. We both came out and spent a moment or two in the area. I suppose our love for Prince refused to die, which was what kept him alive.

Milly and I often think of the strange Carlos Jesus Morales, our so-called shadow world man. He gave us our first intimations about the shadow life, which we thought had to be folkloric and delusional. But why should we have fallen in with it whilst being sceptical and boasting a metaphysical discipline as we still were, despite the evidence being too close to deny? It's all locked up with heaven and hell, angels and after-life legends, and other absurd claims of organized religions.

Through Fire and Brimstone

Private Bradley Cooper and his wife lived up in the Ozark Mountains of Missouri, in a little house Bradley had built with help from his father, who had since passed away. The modest home was from where the marine corporal reported for his tours of duty, first in Iraq and then on a second tour of duty in Afghanistan. He and wife Debra had an understanding that it would be his last, after which he would take his demobilization, come home, and be a good father when the children were born someday. At the time of his departure for Afghanistan, little Kane hadn't yet been born.

Brad and Deb were good, solid, fervent churchgoing Foursquare Gospel Christians. They believed that it was God's wish to face the enemy and keep them from invading America sometime in the future, just as the Reverend Joseph Meyer had been preaching all over the state on Sundays and on any other day if called upon. This was usually during recruitment drives and while blessing recruits who had just graduated from Camp Kennedy on their way to overseas engagements.

The truth is that like most mountain people in the Ozarks, the Coopers were basically decent hard-drinking, hard-working, peace-loving patriotic people who lived in peace with their neighbours. They were generous to all strangers who passed their way and might have been in want of food and water.

While their husbands were away, their wives who lived in and around the small rural town of Fateful, close by where the Coopers lived, would meet regularly and have themselves parties and comforting gossip sessions. It was all they could do to keep loneliness and their fears away. They loved their menfolk and missed them immensely. These lonely women feared for the safety of their men. The women feared the doom of death and wondered if any of them would be left widowed in the near future. The sisterhood was there to give support and comfort.

It was soon after Brad's regiment left for Tarin Kowt that Debra found herself pregnant. It was the base where the marine detachment found itself stationed in Oruzgan Province along with the main force of Australian diggers. She immediately informed her parents of the baby's imminent arrival. They were overjoyed and came down right away from neighbouring Arkansas, where they lived. They stayed with Debra and helped her through the birth when the time came. It was a home delivery, and everything went smoothly. Little Kane was born. The hills around the Cooper home resounded with whoopees and other forms of celebrations for weeks. Debra had more friends dropping in with pressies for the bonny little Kane, who was big, strong, kicking, and chortling all the time. He was easy to love.

The occasional celebratory gunshot echoed from the hills around. With no real earnestness, Deputy Sheriff Joe

Marshall made casual investigations into these incidents. He knew it was just to celebrate Brad's little boy having been "borned". Hell, he let off a round or two himself, come to that, and he came by for some of the mountain whisky Brad was famous for. No one brewed sterner stuff than that marine corporal Brad Cooper did. And the law wasn't the only representation that was made either. One day the Reverend Joseph Meyer drove up the raw mountain road in his rusty and battered jeep, which he refused to get rid of for something prettier. He stayed for a meal and a couple of glasses of mountain whiskey that spread the spirit of God joyously through him. In exchange for Cooper hospitality, he gave a blessing and a prayer for Brad's safety. Brad would survive and come home safe and sound.

Away in the far-flung Ormuzgan Province of Afghanistan, there had been a lull in hostilities after the Taliban lost over a hundred warriors in a firefight. The troops were getting a break and attending to their wounded and the maintenance of their weapons. The days were as hot as ever. Everyone moved slowly but was ever alert. At the baked clay buildings of Tarin Kowt, the capital, Brad got the news at station call when mail was distributed. He heard Coronel Sergeant Hernandez call his name. He leapt to his feet and pushed his way through the throng of the assembled and hopeful other marines expecting and hoping for news from home. It always lifted his spirits when he read the many letters he got from well-wishers – but most of all from his Debra.

This letter was different. He went into a swoon of rhapsody. A baby boy! He had become a dad. He took himself away from the others and read and reread the letter. Tears rolled down his cheeks. He sat looking out at the shimmer of heat coming off the prefabricated walls all around him. He became filled with an awful spread of homesickness and wanted so much for the month to end, when the marines were to move out to Kabul. Their transport planes would then fly them out from Baghram Airport and back to their loved ones and home. He must stay alive. He must not take any more risks in battle, fighting off ambushes or on patrols. He had to stay alive for his son. It now became his sacred mission. He was seized by a desperation to stay alive.

His mates would have told you that taking awful risks in engagements was out of the question where Bradley Cooper was concerned. It was his second nature, the natural reflexes of a warrior, to be the first to charge the enemy, to show no mercy. Stories about the many Talibs he had shot in combat had now translated in top marine legends. He already sported many medals for distinction in combat, many citations for bravery beyond the call of duty. He seemed to live a charmed life. He had seen his buddies cut down in volleys of bullets; he had held the hands of dying buddies. But they could not kill Corporal Bradley Cooper. Even captains, majors, and colonels spoke to him with a special fondness and respect. It was openly passed around that Corporal Cooper was soon to get his third stripe, promoted to the rank of sergeant. And all through this, Private Cooper remained calm and humble. All he wanted was to get home safely to his wife and son. Kane was a good Ozark sort of name. He liked that. He dreamed of the days to come when he would take his son fishing, swimming, canoeing, and walking the Ozark trails with Debbie, who was herself an outdoors person. That would be life! Real life. Ozark life!

After going through all the preliminaries, such as health and fitness tests, unit debriefing, and meeting with other defence officials, an army truck dropped him off at the foot of the rough red road leading up to his cottage. He was the last one dropped off. The truck drove away in a red dust as Private Bradley Cooper, with his rucksack on his back, trudged his joyful way up to his home. Debbie had been waiting and watching. She had heard a truck pull away, but she still had to finish cooking little Kane's lunch. The boy had been playing outside near the water tank when he saw who he thought was a stranger coming up the road. He ran in and informed his mother of such a rare occasion. He nearly fell when mother let out a whoop, and scooping him up in one movement, she ran down to the soldier, who had now reached the steps of the house.

It took a while for the three to disentangle themselves and begin walking into the house. Kane was in his father's arms. It was all so strange to be handled by the man whom he was told was his father. But he soon adjusted to it, played with him, and found a strange rapport building up into what was the beginning of love.

Debra promised to have lunch ready in a minute. In the fridge, there was still all that pie and salad she had prepared the previous night. Brad went into the bedroom and threw himself on to the comfortable bed. This was soon going to be a high altar of some lovemaking. He threw his rucksack on the floor. Kane joined him on the bed. Brad and Kane rolled about on the bed having a lot of fun. Kane had never experienced such happiness before. He really loved this man he had already begun calling Daddy. But Daddy was exhausted, such as he had never been before, not even during battle time, when he found it hard to get much shut-eye. He emptied his pockets, took off his wristwatch, wallet, and sidearm he had been allowed to bring home. He soon fell asleep.

Debra was about to shout "Come and get it!" There were going to be many, many more such calls to the table from now on. She was going crazy with the prospects of a joyous future at last. Her lover boy had come through combat, through what Rev Meyer had called all that fire and brimstone, and he was to be safe forevermore.

Debra had been talking all this time to someone who was asleep. Then she heard his snoring and smiled to herself. Naturally. He must be tired and in need of sleep. What was Kane doing by himself in the bedroom? she wondered. His lunch was also ready.

A shot rang out.

It reverberated through the Ozark hills outside where the house stood. It frightened Debra, who let the glass water jug fall and shatter. The water splattered all over the floor. She ran into the bedroom.

Brad lay dead.

What none of the hundreds of enemy soldiers and armies of fanatical killers failed to do, a four-year-old, his firstborn, his son, Kane, managed on the very day that Corporal Cooper returned home from the wars.

She saw Brad with nearly half his head shot off. Blood filled the bed covers and pillows. The inquisitive boy had somehow gotten hold of the sidearm and had been playing with it, and in the process, he had accidentally slipped off the safety catch and pulled the trigger. He was so stunned that he hadn't raised a yell. He was stunned with fear about the loud explosion he'd created. He had been hurled far across the bed. A lot of his father's blood covered his face. His howling rent the peace of the small house. His was the wailing of one damned forever.

Debra fainted and collapsed on the bedroom floor.

Just then, the telephone began to ring.

The Harsha Vision

I grabbed a trolley and went into the Coles fruit and veggie area. I had only five minutes. We had to be meeting up with friends in the next half hour in Booragoon. Phoenix was about twenty minutes away. It threatened to be a very tight schedule. I planned to fly about picking up whatever I could find and then meet my wife, who was at Lennards … or at least so she said. The usual shoppers were going about in their bored and mesmerized way.

I saw him come through the cavernous mouth of the interior with a fresh load of fruit. He was a new boy on the block – couldn't be more than a week on the job. I knew most of the others on sight, some by their first names. I had done most of what I had been detailed to do, or so I thought, so I decided I'd have a chat with him, as is my wont whenever I see a new African or Asian. I'm not a racist. I like making friends with these newcomers to my country. I like being asked why I consider myself not a racist. That's a long story. We'll pass on that here. So I sidled up to him with my best disarming smile, which some say is frightening.

"Hi. How are you?" I asked.

"I'm OK, thanks," he replied, returning my smile.

"You're new here, aren't you?" I asked.

"Yah." (They all love to say "yah" for some reason. Try it sometime and you'll see!) "This is only my second week."

"What's your name, by the way?"

"Harsha."

"So, where are you from, Harsha?" I asked, screwing up my eyes and peering at his name tag. Interesting name that. I remembered reading about Harsha the Great, an Indian king in Northern India, when I was in school.

"India," he said almost apologetically. I wished he could have been more assertive and somewhat proud having a name like that. He continued stacking some bananas but smiling as if he would like me to stay and chat.

"Aha. So where are you from in the lovely country of India?" I wished I didn't sound so patronizing. I hated talking like that and sounding phoney. I hoped he didn't care that he had to put up with such a jackass.

"Hariyana," he said.

"So you must be a Punjabi," I said, trying to sound prescient.

"No. I am a Hariyani," he corrected me. That put me in my place.

"Yes, but it was once part of Punjab," I said, trying to gain a little cred.

"Oh, so you know a little about my country."

"Of course," I replied magnanimously, flinching with the "little" implication. "I am also Indian."

He dropped the three oranges he was about to put down and stared at me. "No, surely not." He smiled incredulously. This had happened hundreds of times, let me tell you. It always amused me. "How is it possible, sir?"

"That's a long story, I'm afraid," I said.

"Sorry, sir. I'd better get on with my work. I wasn't prying." He seemed flustered. He hurriedly arranged some more oranges, looking anxiously around him.

I picked over some Santa Rosa plums. I had an absolute passion for the juicy black plums. I filled a plastic bag with a week's supply.

I wasn't done with Harsha just yet. "Are you alone in WA, Harsha?" I asked with the kindest tone I could manage.

"No. My wife is with me. We got married seven weeks ago."

"How nice for you. Did you go back to Haryiana to find a wife?"

"No, I found her here in Perth. She is WA born and bred and educated." He smiled proudly. "She did her high school in Governor Stirling and is now an accountancy graduate from Edith Cowan University."

"Her people must be from Haryiana also, I suppose," I said.

"No. They were from Bangladesh."

"Bangladesh? But there aren't any Hindus in Bangladesh. It's a conservative Muslim country," I said, a bit confused by it all.

"Yes, you are right. She's Muslim." He smiled enigmatically.

I was stunned. I stood stupefied. The mango I had been inspecting fell from my hand. He retrieved it with a smile and returned it to me.

"What you are telling me is an impossibility these days," I said.

"She goes to the mosque whenever she feels like it, and I visit our temple in Canning Vale," he said in a casual way, as if it were the most natural thing to do.

"Do the Muslims know that she married a Hindu?" I asked.

"Oh, yes, sir. She isn't the only Muslim woman with a Hindu husband, by the way. We know a Muslim man who has a Russian wife," he explained.

"Well, what can I say after that amazing revelation? A stunning victory for inter-religious harmony and acceptance. How wonderful. I wish we could tell everyone about it. It seems as if the only non-believers the Muslims want to kill are Christian."

"That I can't say yes or no to, sir. I don't know. We just want to live quietly for each other and raise a family here in WA, which we both love," he said with quiet assertion.

What a simple act of faith. I hoped that it would become more widespread throughout the world. Simple but strong people were setting the example for others. This was the answer to sectarian suspicions, hate, and violence.

I realized that I had been taking up too much of his time. It was time for me to let him alone to finish his job before he was told off for wasting time.

This was a wonderful vision of an integrated and loving answer to life.

I looked at my watch. Damn! We weren't going to make it in time to meet up with the Vassallos in Booragoon. I pulled out my cell phone, rang my wife, and told her about being late. I got a very irate wife who said that I had to learn to meet my obligations more conscientiously. She was going to be very embarrassed. What eventuated became an anticlimax. When we were in Booragoon waiting at the Coffee Club, we got a call from the Vassalos, apologizing for not being there but saying they were going to have to call off the meeting. They were very sorry and hoped we would forgive them for the change of plans. They would explain when next we met.

That stole the thunder from my wife's mood. She lamented the loss of what promised to be a fine day out. I didn't mind.

I had had my fine day out, which had been given to me quite inadvertently by Harsha, the manager of the fruit and veggie section of Coles. Nothing would be allowed to take that from me. I had discovered not merely a sweet love story but had felt a creeping in of a cautious optimism. Was this a sign of things to come? It seemed to have the beginnings of another story.

The Sarangi Player of Sago Lane

We had returned to Singapore after an absence of some twenty years. So much had changed: more elegant condos for those who could afford them; the highly ornamental freeway into the city; every kilometre landscaped with red, mauve, and orange bougainvilleas and multi-hued and elegantly green shaped hedges, all adding to the aesthetic appeal that was Singapore. The taxi ride into the central business district was a delight. Before we knew it, we were had arrived at Clark Quay. We have a passion for Clark Quay and the Mandarin Court hotel, which was home for us when we are in Singapore.

Milly and I hurriedly checked into the Swissotel Merchant Court Hotel, and after a shower and some coffee, we headed into Chinatown. We wasted no time getting reacquainted with the island state. The excitement was palpable. The whole island was alive and throbbing with excitement. At least for us it was.

Many years ago, the Chinese had built a beautiful temple, and each subsequent year, something new was added to it, embellishing it and renewing a new and splendid look. It showed how devoted the Buddhists were to their Buddha.

The highly ornate Temple of the Buddha Tooth in the heart of the district of Chinatown had been an enriching addition. We happily breathed in the quixotic spice-laden air.

The Singaporeans didn't do things by halves. This was once the Street of the Dead. It had originally housed the hospice for poor Chinese, where relatives could buy candles, joss sticks, funeral clothes, and cheap coffins. Not that there weren't dying poor Chinese anymore in the new affluent Singapore, but they were now obliged to die out of sight somewhere else.

Much of old Chinatown had been demolished in 1961, and a carefully planned new heart was built in 1972. This was a sort of commercialization of death in the new Singapore. Perhaps I am being a bit too critical, maybe even a bit envious of the island state – I don't know. Maybe. But the current landscape was a strange admixture of lovely modern towering complexes that formed a backdrop for the ultra-modern commercial world of affluence. Against this was set the lovely quintessential Chinese old-world architecture. Past and present had learnt to coexist in a happy compromise.

Shamelessly we did the touristy thing. We gawped around the place to satisfy the eyes, ears, and nose as we drank in the charm of Sago Street and the new temple. I wandered about peering at all the things for which the natives were shopping. Milly loved the trinkets and baubles, often exclaiming her delight and imploring my attention. I tended not to get too excited except when I knew it would please her. Then I would oblige with a supporting "ooh!" or an "aah!"

We loved brushing shoulders with the teeming masses, especially in Chinatown and Little India. We picked our way through the shopping crowd that day near the Buddhist temple. This was when I heard the quaint and what I thought somewhat disordered strain of stringed music. I ignored it for a little while, but wherever I turned, it was there. A quaint stringy sound, it produced a sort of plaintive melody that was new to us. Milly held my arm and asked me if I could detect from where the music was emanating. She looked around and pointed out the sarangi player who sat on a low stool. The sarangi was a crude-looking two-string musical instrument which was played with a bow.

Our sarangi player, to all outward appearances, was an ancient, toothless, yellowing ancient Chinaman whose desiccated and wrinkled skin gave him the appearance of an animated relic, his skin as old as parchment. He obviously enjoyed what he was doing, playing his music for his part of the world to listen to. So we paid him the tribute of what was a five-minute audience. He appreciated it because he smiled even more. This exposed the toothless gap that was meant to be a smile. We smiled back. We enjoyed the interlude. So did he. He was part of the music as much as the music was a part of him. It touched a part of me that made my trip to Singapore an event whose memory I would always cherish in a special way. My sarangi player and his music meant more than I would have been able to put into words if anyone asked me to. I had thought about the old musician many times after that.

At that moment, I felt his wise old eyes go deep into me. It had a hypnotic quality I found a bit eerie, and it filled me with a quiet unease for some reason. I smiled back at him. He nodded, and then he nodded again. I took it as a sort of invitation that he wanted to meet me. I caught myself up and chided myself that I was being presumptuous, doing the typical touristy thing. I felt that I was being a bit arrogant, a bit patronising. After all, there was no reason why he would want to acquaint himself with an Australian tourist. It would be the height of bad manners to give him some money, and even if I wanted to, it was a problem as to how much would be an acceptable amount so that it would not be insulting to him. He had a dignity that was beholden of me to respect.

I turned away to see what Milly wanted me to see. A shop was displaying several brightly coloured beautiful silk scarves, all so exotic and subtle. I knew they were of the kind that Milly loved and for which she was always on the lookout. I heard what turned out to be more than a cackle. It was a laugh. His laughter was a dry cackle. He stopped playing and looked up to address us.

"Hullo, Uncle. How are you?" he asked.

It was often a feature of Asian greeting for certain elderly foreigners. I believe it was a hangover from a colonial past. But why "uncle"? It was a throwback to the imperial period of the Raj, I thought.

We were both surprised and pleased he chose to speak to us.

"Thank you. We are fine," I replied. "How are you?"

"I am an old man. Sometimes up. Sometimes down," he replied with a laugh. "You come to Singapore to buy or have happy time?" he asked.

"Maybe a bit of both," Milly replied truthfully.

He nodded and scraped out a few more bars on his sarangi. "You know what this is?" he asked, holding out the stringed instrument.

"A sarangi," replied Milly, who recognized it from the times she had spent in rural India.

This pleased the old man. It brought a light into his eyes. I thought it cemented a certain bond between us. It was unusual knowledge coming from materialistic foreigners. He must have found it gratifying that one should be somewhat familiar with something of the island culture. He smiled and nodded, but he held out his right hand as if he would detain us.

"It is much more, my friend. This is the link to the world I knew as a child. It brings my childhood into this year, twenty ten. It is a time machine." He chuckled, laughing the way an old man would.

"My body feels like it is the body of an old man, full of pain and disease. My heart feels like the heart of a child, full of the music my mother and father brought into my life. You like it?"

We hastened to agree that we did. I felt I should try to tell him what it meant to me, but I knew it meant as much to Milly, whose childhood had been spent in rural Bihar, where she and her family were the only Christians who lived there. The Indian connection was still very strong in her. It held only the merest tenuous hold on me, however. But I was still appreciative of this cultural icon.

The three of us fell silent with this quietly delivered comment. I felt the magic of his simple wisdom pass over me like a benediction. It made me feel suddenly humble. I wondered how this chance meeting with a Chinese minstrel could bring us sharply and unexpectedly with a part of our past. It was quite revealing how differently we both reacted. This was what we discussed over dinner later that night.

"Thank you for your time, sir," I said.

"Enjoy your life, friend. Never lose the child in your heart," he added slowly. "Listen to the music of your past life and clasp tightly the gems of wisdom of your inheritance."

Was there some insight that made him utter these strange and intriguing words? I stood looking at him in wonder at what had just transpired. Was it possible that our souls had been in some kind of intuitive communication, likeness calling to likeness? I was finding it difficult to cope with this explosion that had the energy of an epiphany. I was in denial; surely not. Why not? I argued back and forth in the few moments that enfolded us both.

He returned to his sarangi and played as if we weren't there any longer. Nor was he. He seemed to have passed into a trance, so deeply immersed was he in his music.

This was nothing like the Singapore we thought we'd find. This was no longer the world of towering chrome and glass twenty-first-century ultra-modern urbanization. Modernity was suddenly so far away, and here was a history that lingered in all its fairy-tale romance and yearning for the past. We had momentarily been transported to a world we couldn't define but which wasn't quite alien at the same time. We had it in each of us when we were children, unknown to each other, hundreds of miles apart but drawn together into this shared experience here in Sago Lane, where the times, past and present, intersected.

The Fifth Horseman of the Apocalypse

Long after the logging industry lost its future in the gigantic legal battles in the Supreme Court, they abandoned the lumber town someone had named Adolphus in the massive clearing they had gouged out in the middle of the karri land on the western slopes of the Darling escarpment that ran down steeply into Bunbury.

Adolphus almost became a ghost town of three hundred people, whereas it had once boasted a population of over nearly one thousand. There still stood the old town hall and shire office, both all the worse for a lack of fresh paint. The pharmacy, it was said, only dispensed Panadol, Bethedine, and Dettol. The police station was probably the most vulnerable of public-funded institutions, as it barely escaped audits, thus escaping closure. Senior Constable Smith returned to it every now and then from his excursions around the town. He lived with his wife in a cottage five kilometres from the town centre. At times, outside the ramshackle police office, he could be seen tinkering with the aging police car that had seen more action locating crashed cars and chasing forlornly after speeding youths. Carl from the nearby Star service station often ambled in to lend a hand if Smith ran into difficulties with maintenance work.

More importantly, the town claimed two churches that served the spiritual needs of the town. The Church of the Good Shepherd was for the Roman Catholics, and the Anglican St Michael and All Angels competed for what remained of the rest who rambled into church on Sundays.

Father Pasquarelli, all of seventy years of age and refusing retirement, was the spiritual comforter to his flock. Over 75 per cent of the population in Adolphus were Catholics. These were the remnants of the logging community that stayed on after the others had been laid off or gone to seek their fortunes in Bunbury or farther afield. They managed to find work in a slowly growing hospitality business as more and more people responded to some aggressive and brilliant public relation work and advertising. Others had help starting up industries run from their homes. It had become noticeable that some buildings were sporting fresh coats of bright paint.

One day Father Pasquarelli unexpectedly found himself playing host to the mysterious Father Jasper, who brought with him a special letter of reference from the bishop of Bunbury. Pasquarelli was advised that Father Jasper was not to have any role in the church choir or preparation of children for any ritual or community activity. He was always to wear his white habit with hood complete. This was to remind him constantly of his holy calling and to make him a marked man. Accordingly, the newcomer was called in, and the letter was read to him. Advice was offered in the sternest manner.

The congregation was not informed of these requirements, but it was noticed that he slipped in and out of mass and did not bother to have anything to do with anyone. He seemed very much the loner, highly secretive and reclusive.

At time, he was seen in the fringe of the karri forest or sitting beside the river that burbled by near the church, always with a book in hand. No one knew just what it was that he read. Christmas and Easter found him entering into a meditation session with a visiting priest. They held long sessions alone in the rectory and by the river.

It happened that one day Father Jasper sat on his favourite rock by the river. There were a few trees towering above and a plethora of bushes around him. On this occasion, he suffered from a form of spiritual fatigue, so he decided to give himself a break. He put his book down and wiped his brow with a cloth. As he put the cloth into his pocket, his eyes began to focus on a face some distance from where he sat. The man sat peering into his face. He made no movements at all. He sat still, simply gazing. It struck the priest as being more than merely odd; it was very mysterious. They formed a silent tableau for some time, during which the priest heard a bee fly cross his face. He swatted it away. Some insect bit him on his hand. Nearby, a small creature rustled in the bushes.

Something about the man tugged at his memory, but it held no recognition of him or anything that may have been associated with him. The priest grew restless, strangely enough. The situation bred a vulnerability with which he did not know how to deal.

The stranger never batted an eyelid all this time but continued to stare emotionlessly and fixed on what he may have been intending. He watched the priest begin to change subtly. What had been a mild surprise soon became a perplexed look. Time transformed it into something that passed for concern. Even now, after all that time, neither chose to say anything by way of greeting, recognition, or challenge.

It was Father Jasper who broke first with a whispered inquiry: "Yes?" He hoped that would start a conversation that would reveal the person and his purpose for coming here and why he had chosen to create what could only be interpreted as a sort of mystery.

"Father Jasper," he said. It wasn't a question; it was a statement of identification. It held a sense of finality. The tone held only the merest edge of an accusation. It was quite casual and yet … it made the mystery for the priest even deeper.

"Do … I … know … you?" the priest asked with a stammer.

The man kept silent again, but now only for a little while. He seemed to be playing a subtle but unsettling game with Father Jasper.

"And so you should, Father," said the man. He drew himself up to his full height, which was nothing unusual. He was of average build, slightly balding in a way that wasn't immediately noticeable.

Father Jasper was now fully alert but still somewhat mystified. Something told him that he should be able to recognize him, but the person he was beginning to resemble was still uncertain. The "Father" bit was not lost on him. It lent a stab of fear in his heart. A tremor ran through his body. It was clearly meant to help him recognize him. And now it did.

Father Jasper slowly approached the man he thought was a stranger. He came closer, face-to-face, and reached out his right hand to his face. He ran his fingers over the stubble on the man's face. He peered into his eyes with astonishment and some trepidation.

"Joshua Ashenden?" he asked uncertainly, although even as he asked his question he knew he was right. He felt the years fall away. He drew a sharp breath. Joshua raised his hand in a return gesture and touched the hand of the priest.

"Yes, Father," he whispered.

Both men appeared uncertain as to what should be said or done now that the identifications were completed.

Father Jasper made the first move. He retreated to the rock where he'd once sat and stared down at the earth. Incredulity washed over his haggard face. "How on earth did you find me?" he asked. "It should never have happened."

"I don't know if you remember Carlos Monteiro, but he passed through Adolphus some time ago on a feasibility study, being in the business of opening up little-known places for tourism," said Joshua. "He works for the State Bureau of Tourism now. Well, he thought I should know right away, and last month he found out where he could get in touch with me. He managed to find me after some inquiries. He swore that he had caught a glimpse of you here. Of course, I wanted to find out for myself. So that is how I managed to come over despite a marked reluctance to open up the past we both must find so painful." His voice fell away so that the last bit barely managed to reach the priest, who raised his eyes slowly to meet Joshua's gaze.

"This is what happens to paedophile priests. We are shifted and hidden as far as possible to escape the law. You and I have already talked this over before this, Joshua," the priest said, looking away into the bush.

"You are no paedophile, Father. I grew up loving you as if you were the father I never knew because he abandoned us after beating us almost insensible after his worst drunken rage. Mother nearly died. You were the only one who stood by us and saved us.

"Don't you remember all that happened to separate us in those years?" His voice broke. He choked back a sob.

"You loved me and I loved you," he continued. "Now I hear that you went too far with some others. How can this be, my father? You loved me and cared for me. I don't know why, but I want to love you still, and I crave your love. Don't you love me? How could you be what others are calling you?"

The afternoon light was beginning to retreat into growing shadows. In this opening in the bush near the old church, it seemed charged with an emotional atmosphere that was foreign to its usual benign air. The priest's body heaved, and he began sweating profusely.

Father Jasper nodded his head and acknowledged the tragedy that he took personally. His pastoral responsibilities had demanded he step in and bring salvation to this battered family. The memories were still very fresh. A relationship developed between him and the boy, who broke away whenever he could to visit Father Jasper, who delicately tried to caution the boy against too many open visits. The atmosphere of a running witch-hunt to expose paedophilia in parishes made it all very uncomfortable. In exile, he recounted the sad and immoral history of the past. He now knew that innocence itself wasn't enough to ward off the odium attached to such delicate and open effusions of affection. Not when the rest of what happened destroyed that innocence. What a piece of work was man, part saint and part beast.

The climax was reached the day Joshua visited him near the grotto. He found the priest very agitated and fearful. He asked the boy to return home quickly. He wasn't well. But the boy became a victim to the relationship and instead offered to get a doctor. When Father Jasper took hold of his shoulders and demanded he do no such thing but go home there and then, Joshua, overcome by the moment and deeply moved by his friend's suffering, suddenly leant over the kneeling priest and kissed him. As fate would have it, the Bishop happened to be passing that way, and he was rooted to the spot. Father Jasper had betrayed his trust and the forgiveness he had offered Father Pasquarelli for three previous indiscretions of a similar nature, though really even worse, but unknown to Joshua.

Pasquarelli had to act promptly now and send Jasper away, just as he had exiled two other offenders. Jasper had again betrayed his calling. He had no choice in the matter. He was aware of the mood of the public and the attention the police were now giving the churches. There was talk of a commission being set up by the federal government to look into all accusations from as far back as half a century. The Roman Catholic had heard the hoof beats of that dreaded new fifth horse of the Apocalypse that had appeared to herald the death of the now moribund and corrupted establishment that had once embarked on the holy mission of service and redemption of the world. Over two thousand priests had been transformed into paedophile monsters that had sexually abused thousands of innocent children all around the world. Some of these monsters were bishops and cardinals. Hundreds of churches had been bankrupted, and millions of parishioners were now without paschal aid and the ritualistic care the church had a duty to offer. In disillusionment, many had ceased attending mass and were now numbered amongst the atheists of the world.

"I'm sorry for you, Jasper. Please try to forgive me and try to forget the entire sorry episode in my rotten life. I am beyond redemption. I belong to the legion of the damned. Goodbye," whispered Father Jasper, pausing by Joshua's side as he made his way out of sight.

Joshua stood alone for some time and stared down into the undergrowth, where unconcerned little creatures went about their daily life untroubled, where no betrayal or sense of guilt and anger threatened the harmony of their world. He reacted strongly to a sense of rejection. The loss of yet another father under tragic circumstances touched him very much. So much hung upon forgiveness and a happy reconciliation. He would endure the odium of his father's present shame. They could see it through and be there for one another. A new life had looked possible … for a brief time. He slowly walked back to his red BMW to go home.

Later in the day, somewhere round sunset, word came to the Bunbury traffic police that there had been a fatality down the steepest section of the Vasse Highway. A car had gone over the top and plunged over one hundred metres down the slope, where it had burst into flames. The driver was unidentifiable. The vehicle had been a red BMW.

The Coolies

The skies were black. Thunder rumbled just over the horizon. Every now and then, the black pall would get riven by bluish forked lightning that was accompanied by the loudest claps of thunder, making the world shudder. For now, the torrential monsoon rains had stopped falling, returning the world to a strained calm.

A few passengers at the station languished in the humidity and vainly sought to cool themselves by fanning themselves. Dhullian Bagh was a small divisional station with a limited staff and little or no public facilities.

The stationmaster had vacated his office to the regional railway controller, Bruce Smith, who had been asked by the CEO of the division to reprimand Public Works Department in-charge James Lester, who had only recently been promoted to the job. The CEO had asked him to send ten coolies to his house to help in the unloading of furniture recently purchased in Calcutta. What had transpired was unforgivable. PW Inspector Lester replied that he had no coolies under him. His staff members were not coolies; they were human beings, trolley men. Everyone needed to remember that. For this affront, he was to receive the sternest of reprimands along with a warning for dismissal if his attitude didn't change.

The reprimand having been duly delivered, Controller Smith asked what the bloody hell he had meant by that, and Lester had informed him that he had no coolies under him but only a trolley crew of ten runners. The meeting had concluded with the controller speaking informally, saying, "For God's sake, Jim, pull your head in. Don't jeopardize your position. Just go with the flow. No more smart aleck stuff and don't take on the authority on such frivolous points."

"I'm glad you can see it as that, sir," said Lester as he was allowed to go.

He went out and found six of his crew waiting apprehensively to see him. News had come down the line. It was bad news. Senior Trolley man, Gautam Das, was dying. They should be on their way as soon as possible to see him before he passed away and help his wife, Devi, and their little son, Ram.

The PW Inspector looked at the sky and warned them that it could be very dangerous if any more rain fell. The rail line could be under water soon. They begged him to try it anyway. They were willing to risk their own families' future too if the sahib was willing to risk his own life. They felt that they were all one family.

"OK, then get the trolley back on line and put all your gear and tools on as well," said PWI Lester. "Hurry. I have a bad feeling about the coming storm. Hurry."

Soon the trolley was again humming along its twin silver tracks and racing home, powered by a set of eight thin but wiry legs of the runners who hurled the machine to go as fast as it could.

Suddenly, around a bend, the sounds and sight of the raging River Kosi came into awesome view. It was overflowing its banks. The tracks had been raised on top of a levee, or bund as it was known. The brown swirling waters lapped the rails in places, and it was only the incredible running balance sense of the trolley men that enabled them to negotiate the rails, but only by having to slow down a bit. Their officer made a note of what he was seeing, the usual flood detritus of tree branches that had been torn away from trees. There were also carcasses of drowned cattle. He also saw at least four bloated corpses. Fortune favoured the brave. Only a few light drops of rain fell, threatening much more about to follow. The men well knew this and urged their tiring feet to give more run. In this way, the trolley finally made Chapra, and then it was home at last. Orders were given to secure the trolley and all equipment and proceed right away to Gautam Das's house, as if the urging were really necessary. In the meantime, the PWI went to his office and made out his routine way inspection notes, then made his way to Gautam Das's village. He knew where he lived.

Gautam Das had been dead some hours. Relatives and friends were at the house, adding to the wailing and hysteria. Word got out that the sahib was outside. Thereupon the widow ran, hair streaming wildly, holding fast to the hand of her son, Ram Das, who was crying. She threw herself at the feet of their visitor. She held his feet and stared into his feet.

"Tell me, Lester sahib, now what am I to do? There is no food in the house. I have little or no money to buy any. What there is must go to paying for the funeral of my good man, Gautam. What is to become of me and my son, Ram Das? Please have mercy on us. Do something, please," she begged pitifully, gazing into the face of the sahib."

PWI Lester was lost in a flood of sadness, and in considerable confusion. This was the first such situation he had ever encountered. He was very conscious of family, of doing all he could to save it, but what that could be he wasn't sure. All his education in Dr Graham's Homes was on sharing responsibilities with everyone and helping family. He instinctively saw before him a family facing dissolution.

No sooner had the widow fallen at his feet than he quickly stooped and picked her up. He put up his hand to restore some order and quieten the howling. Gradually it took hold, although the sobbing could not be snuffed out. He looked around and found Bhai Ram, his second in command. He beckoned him. Taking Ram Das by the hand, he ordered him to put him on the payroll. He was to replace his father with immediate effect.

Bhai Ram blinked at what he saw as an error in authority. The lad was too young to be a trolley man. To point this out now at this point of proceeding was too much for him as his eyes went to the widow. He knew of her circumstances. Gautam owed money to a couple of workers. But employment for Ram Das was out of the question.

He cleared his throat and felt compelled to say out loud, "But, sir, we cannot do that. The lad isn't yet …"

But the voice of the sahib cut him short. "Ram Das is now fourteen years of age, the age that apprentices can be put on the payroll. I am on my way right now to see the munshi and order him to officially register a replacement for Gautam Das. I have the authority to do this. Don't worry about it. I know what I am doing. You will take the lad aside and prepare him as to what he should say and do. Everyone will help him to learn the foot running skills of a runner trolley man."

There was a ripple of approval. Some hailed him as a god. Such exaggerated sentiments were quite common with the villagers in these parts of the land. Voices thanked the sahib, and some reached down to touch his feet. The sahib pushed himself away and asked the widow to follow him to the station. Her aging parents and a few other relatives accompanied her. She was to get monetary aid as a loan which he had no intentions of making Ram Das repay. The "loan" would all find its way mysteriously into Ram Das's hands without anyone being any the wiser.

When they returned to where the trolley had been banked, the weather seemed to let up. A streak of sunlight lit up the little station and the shiny twin rails running away into the distance. Another train was on its way in, and work had to return to normal quickly and efficiently.

Yellow Bird

His eyesight was gradually fading. His limbs were getting hard to use without pain. His hearing needed a lot of adjusting because he found it hard to separate the sounds that were important to him and which he strove to catch and separate from the sounds the world afflicted upon him.

Every morning, as early as possible, he made his way down to the shore. The water's edge ran foaming ripples around his gnarled feet. He loved to feel the frothy wavelets tickle his toes, and he smiled them a greeting. He stood staring out at the clouds gathering at the horizon. He knew that the day would come when he may not be able to see them at all. He listened to the breakers bringing their watery secrets from lands far, far away, lands with strange-looking people with their strange-sounding names. The day would come when he may not get to hear the music of the ocean as clearly as he would like.

What was even sadder would be the song of his yellow bird that would waft down from the trees under which he would sit for hours listening so intently. He would then join in softly, singing the words he had made up many years ago when she was alive with him. They made up their own song of life. That ended many years ago. In his memory, he still heard them softly sing the song to each other. Now she was no longer here, but the yellow bird sang to him to make up for the voice that life had cruelly stilled. When he heard the song of the yellow bird, he heard her singing and joined in, as he did now.

The forest closed him round as he walked away from the shore. Dry twigs snapped and crackled underfoot. He went to the favourite tree of the yellow bird and looked up into the dense foliage. Now and again, he saw the bird flit about from branch to branch. It was looking for food. The old man followed its movements and waited and waited. He got tired so he sat down to rest. He still gazed upwards, but the bird seemed to ignore him. He smiled his acceptance. He knew how stubborn the bird could be at times. He sat down to listen. The forest seemed to listen as well. Gradually fatigue took hold and the old man stretched his frail body on the forest floor.

Everyone knows at some time or another how peaceful hope and a moment it brings with it can feel. The forest, however, gazed upon its own primeval promise of Edenesque home and exhaled its silent lamentations in the humidity through the green canopy and below it, where animal and birds sweltered, as did human beings who went no farther than where they made their forest home. They never asked how it came about that the forest and sea became their part of the world. It was enough to accept that this became home for them as it had for their ancestors and their distant ancestors down the dim ages of their history. It was enough for their simple minds to cope with the several challenges of life.

Then a sharp beautiful musical sound drifted down from some treetop. It was cut short. Then it was repeated … and ended as abruptly. A longer silence settled in. The recumbent figure of the old man moved. He raised himself on an elbow and stared into the streams of forest light. He waited intently and caught the sound of the yellow bird, but it came from farther, deeper in the interior.

The truth was that the bird had not really flown any distance away from where it had had first been seen. The old man's sense of hearing was suddenly growing weaker for some reason, but he didn't quite realize it. Death has a way of creeping up unheralded some times. Maybe it was better that way, when it felt like a gentle sleep. Then it held no fears for any creature. A rare light came into the old man's eyes, as if making one last final attempt to offer him a chance to view the retreating world.

His singing could be heard as it softly but joyously wafted up and out into the tree where the yellow bird had come for him.

> *Yellow bird, sitting alone in the mango tree.*
> *Yellow bird, all alone,*
> *Sitting all alone in the mango tree.*
> *All alone in the world like me.*

All the while unseen by him, the ocean had been filling the sky above with moisture that grew large, high white castles, menacing and turning black. This happened about the same time every day. Suddenly, the clouds would violently light up the sky as fiery fingers searched for anything in the way. Loud claps of thunder would crash upon the world below and echo many times through the forest. The world would grow very still and quiet. Rain poured heavily for an hour or so, washed the entire canopy below, and gave sustenance to the plant life below. All living creatures panicked and looked for cover. Sheets of water washed away the dirt on treetops, on the earth below, and on most living things that may have been caught below.

> *Yellow bird, all alone,*
> *Will you come looking for me?*

Silence poured down from the trees.

The yellow bird grew silent in deference to the power nature had unleashed in the world above. It hid itself wherever trees offered it safety. It stayed hidden until the sun burst through the heavy curtain that had hidden it all afternoon. Eventually, the creatures of the forest began calling each other to see if all were well again. The rain had passed over. Leaf tops sparkled like millions of diamonds, and for a time, droplets of water fell below.

The old man lay very still. One more time his dimmed eyes opened. He blinked away the droplets that had managed to get in. He heard the yellow bird above. He was also able to see it one more time because it had flown down from its arboreal refuge. Its singing swelled out to make sure the man heard it. The old man smiled sadly in response. The man tried to smile as he gently accompanied it:

> *Yellow bird, sitting alone in the mango tree.*
> *Yellow bird, all alone,*
> *Sitting all alone like me …*

This song does not end. It will always be heard by those who have a special ear for ethereal singing, for those who live close to this special world. The singer had merely fallen asleep. He no longer moved. The bird flitted from branch to branch, from tree to tree.

It sang above the old man.

> *I will always come to sing our song.*
> *I will always sing this song for you.*

As the day wore on, the people of the village began to worry and made up a search party to look for him. It wasn't hard to locate him. It was much later in the day that the men, women, and children of the tribe came down and gathered vines and palm fronds to make a litter for his body to bear him away with them. As was the custom, they set up a rhythmical chanting reserved specially for the dead. The body in the litter swayed gently as he was returned to his people and their ancestors. The world went on without him.

The Panchgani-Pune Express

Ana Rasmussen was into her final week in India. She was a final year student in the Royal Copenhagen Institute of Technology. She had taken a year off to do research into Danish missions in India. There weren't many such missions, so she had time to study the social mores of the women of India. Her work had taken her from Simla in the north to Trivandrum in the south. She was advised by friends to visit the lovely hill station of Panchgani that nestled on the edge of the western ghat escarpment that was formed by basaltic extrusions that had bubbled out from the bowels of the earth hundreds of thousands of years ago and now formed plateaux.

She'd come to love the serene hamlet which was home to some dozen schools that littered the plateau country and which were open nine months of the year. The schools nearly doubled the population of Panchgani during the school terms. She was able to visit some of them and was impressed by what she saw. The schools were elitist and expensive, but the parents were all affluent and more than happy to patronise the schools. The students were bright and cheerful and clearly loved their schools.

But now it was time to keep her appointment at the Danish trade commissioner's office in Mumbai before embarking on an Air India flight home. She barely made it as the bus began to roll out of Panchgani. She ran screaming for them to wait. She waved her hands about desperately. Bystanders were helpful in alerting the driver, who stopped obligingly with a broad smile.

There was only one seat left, and it was near the right rear window, where a blanketed figure sat and peered out of the window. After making herself as comfortable as possible, Ana began an attempt to begin some sort of a conversation, but the person clearly preferred to remain shrouded and ignored her, whimpering softly now and then, so Anna got out a packet of sandwiches that friends had brought her for her journey. She unwrapped it and thought of her neighbour, whose body was still covered completely under a frayed and smelling cotton blanket. She was seized with an urge to offer the person some of her food. She got no response. Perhaps the person preferred her own company, so Anna complied with her assumption. She looked around her and saw smiling faces beaming at her, so she smiled back at them. Everywhere she'd travelled in the subcontinent, she found Indians eager to be friendly. The poorer they were, the happier they seemed. It seemed to be a national trait, a most commendable one. She came to admire and love them.

The journey down the winding ghat to Wai had them clinging to the edges of a dangerous route so Ana was vastly relieved to reach the plains where Wai was located before the long haul to Pune, which was some sixty-odd miles away. They paused for about ten minutes to take on passengers with their market produce. The market in Wai, like all marketplaces in India, was overcrowded. She had enough time to get down and buy a bottle of water. She had learnt not to eat any uncovered food from fast-food sellers in marketplaces. Ana loved the chorus of voices, punctuated by the shrill laughter of children. She found Indian shoppers ever so vibrant. She also found the smell of markets exotic and quite heady. Ana tried to soak up as much of the local atmosphere as possible before resuming each journey. All of this was too rapidly ending, and soon she would be back home. Her mind was jolted back to reality shortly after they lurched forward.

They nearly had an accident shortly after resumption. On their way to Pune, the bus had to swerve to miss a man on a bicycle who had baskets of chickens in finely balanced arrangement on the carrier at the back as he headed out to the market in Wai. The angry cyclist and the Sikh bus driver exchanged heated abuse.

The swerve produced a dramatic revelation for Ana. The blanket round the inert figure next to her slipped off her reclusive neighbour. The shrouded figure was a leper. As the blanket fell away, it revealed a hand that had only stumps for fingers. The terrified leper had a face horribly distorted by the disease. She had a hole in the face for a nose. Her didn't have lips to cover her yellow teeth, and her eyes looked like sightless sockets. Blobs of diseased flesh long since eaten away by the disease seemed to be falling off her head. From the dirty threadbare blanket, a nasty smell filled the fetid air, not that others noticed, or if they did, they chose not to do or say anything about it. It was as if she wasn't there … didn't exist. Such an experience had never confronted Ana previously, and she now felt extremely nauseous. She knew the bus would never stop for her to get air. She leaned as far away as she could from the poor wretch. Ana was overcome with both sadness and fear for herself lest she be contaminated.

Two hours later, when they reached Pune, everyone alighted at the terminal. Packing cases, crates, and bedrolls were collected, and in a short time, no one remained but the cowering figure by the window. The burly Sikh driver checked out the interior of the bus to make sure every passenger had left and that there were no items that may have been forgotten. They would have to be taken into the office. He finally noticed her and roundly abused her and shouted at her. Ana approached him uncertainly and urged him to treat her with some respect. She too was a human being and was especially in need of everyone's love and care. The Sikh driver drew a breath and looked skyward. He had encountered these foreigners before, mostly young backpackers, all so noisy and arrogant. They spoke condescendingly to Indians. They thought all they met were ignorant and socially inferior. He became quite irate. He ignored her and shook off her restraining hand. Ana struggled briefly with him, but he was too strong for her.

He disappeared briefly into an office and re-emerged shortly, producing a pole with a hook at the end with which he tore the fugitive figure of the leper out of the bus and on to the bitumen, where she scampered away like a diseased crab, her blanket trailing her decomposing body.

"Madam, do not interfere. You white foreigners have no idea what this sort of life is that exists in India. I have a responsibility to my company. I could lose my job if anyone found out that I had brought a leper all the way from Panchgani. I have a wife and five children to support. Don't you know how this thing happened?"

He began to walk away dismissively, the contempt in his voice matching his arrogance. Ana trailed in his wake, all the while asking for assistance for the poor leper woman. The Sikh swivelled about in exasperation and faced a perplexed Ana, who didn't know what to think or do.

"This creature's parents or friends or whoever … perhaps relatives … bought her a ticket, and before anyone else could board the bus, secretly put her in a corner and promptly left the depot. No one has met her here at this end, have they? Why do you think? What happens to her now is karma. Come on. I will phone the police for you, all right?"

Ana asked him to call the hospital instead. What could the police do? Ana felt that a little aggression in her tone might help. The Sikh driver said he would call the hospital as well to please her, and he'd call anyone else she cared to name, although he said that he couldn't believe he was going to all this trouble for an interfering white woman. Just then, voices began calling out to the driver to log out and enquiring what the trouble was. The superintendent and another official came over, and he explained what it was all about.

"Madam, I am Superintendent Bhonsle of the Pune Bus Company. I frankly don't see what business this is of yours," he said in a squeaky cracked voice because of his age, but he was obviously determined to pull rank.

"Can't you see the injustice to this poor wretched woman who is suffering enough without the added indignity of such treatment?" Ana hotly retorted.

They looked around for the leper, but she had crawled away in all her pain and hunger into the night, into another hole of hell. Where could she have crawled off to – a sewer to avoid people when the morning broke and wait the approach of merciful death? There was nothing unusual about this. Millions like her lived through death repeatedly.

Meanwhile, the Sikh driver had contacted the police, who berated him for some time and finally asked him if he was mad to call them about a leper. They weren't going to waste their time. Leprosy wasn't a criminal offence.

He next phoned the hospital, only to be told to get in touch with the leper asylum, which was 150 kilometres away. Ana took over the phone and tried to argue her case, but she was told, "Miss, you found her; you do something for her. She is your responsibility now."

Something made Ana look down at her wristwatch. With a gasp, she saw that she had ten minutes left to catch the Pune-Mumbai Mail. She slammed the phone down and ran off as fast as she could, lugging her backpack over her shoulder. She felt like a sad and defeated Samaritan.

In some deserted street in Pune, in a lonely culvert, or under a tree somewhere, a wasted human life was draining away, uncared for, in dreadful pain, in the loneliness of rejection and fear, praying for death. And all the while, the body was quivered and the disease eating away at what remained.

When the God of Death
Is the Death of God

Haiti is the poorest country in the West Indies. It shares an island with the Dominican Republic, which lies to its east. Poverty doesn't prevent the people's fervent adherence to their religions. They love to demonstrate their devotion in song and dance to show their love of God. They have very colourful Creole and musical expressions of faith.

On Tuesday, 12 January 2010, the working day was almost at an end. It was a peaceful day under a fleecy sky, where indolent clouds hovered about lazily. The serenity wasn't to last long. At precisely 4.53 p.m., Haiti jumped about ten centimetres into the air with an ear-splitting roar. An earthquake with a magnitude of seven hit Haiti. Rows of palm trees and all the modest buildings along the beach outside the coastal town of Leogane, twenty-five kilometres west from the capital, Port-au-Prince, came crashing down, and the sea leapt in and with the massive quakes destroyed the town completely. Fishing vessels were washed up more than one hundred metres into the town. That wasn't the worst thing that happened.

It was a very black day when the heart of Haiti was torn apart. The two major spiritual centres, the Anglican Cathedral of the Holy Trinity and the Roman Catholic Cathedral of Our Lady of Assumptions disappeared in a cloud of rubble and accompanying choking dust, only to reappear shortly in heaps of heartbreaking debris and broken prayers. Shattered masonry, a tangle of wrought iron, exposed brickwork, and wooden ribs of heavy timber clawed at the heartless sky above.

Broken bodies of angels, an assortment of saints, and Jesus and Mary could be seen lying about desecrated altars. Despite their own broken bodies and other personal losses, men, women, and children, maimed, bloodied, and covered in dust and grime, ran frantically, wild-eyed and screaming, trying to salvage whatever they thought they should. Some dropped dead because of their brave but fruitless efforts. Amongst the dead was the much-loved Archbishop Joseph Serge Miot. The irate God did not discriminate. He took the powerful and the common, the pious and the sinners, the richest and poorest alike. What was he angry about? No one really knew.

It must have been mostly the poor he didn't much care for, it seemed. The slum city of Cité Soleil was no more. Most of the three hundred thousand who perished were amongst the poorest of this slum, as if there weren't enough of a tragedy whilst they lived. Bodies lay all over the place in various and bizarre poses of their mortality. The stench of death made the capital city stink like a slaughterhouse. Rotting corpses littered the city. Lean uncared-for dogs roamed the ruins and knew where the corpses were.

What clutched at the hearts of most was the sight of schoolchildren who died in play. Skipping ropes were still in the hands of a few, their innocence abused by the coldness of their brutal deaths. Flying sheets of glass had decapitated three who were nearest shops. The heads had rolled some distance away, driven by the impetus of tremors. The eyes and mouth of each head formed a hideous grimace. These children were found in Cité Soleil. There would probably be none to mourn them. Their parents lay dead in their homes or where they worked. That day, over three hundred thousand died horribly. There was to be a mass burial organized by the churches, a further indignity added to the tragedy, but it was inevitable and was the only response possible after a death of such magnitude. Dogs were the only ones who seemed to come out on top. Some were seen eating the choicest sections they could tear off the corpses. Men who had enough energy swore as loudly as they could and threw stones that scared them off. Other dogs were seen dragging off remains of the dead to some secret locations where they could eat in peace and be safe from having their meals disturbed.

Even whilst the survivors and the army, police, and paramedics organized some semblance of cleaning up, getting rid of rubble, restoring order, and pulling the dead and wounded out of wrecked buildings, the ground kept trembling, shock after shock, bringing down those parts of buildings that managed to hang on precariously to their parent structures. Some people lost their balance, whilst others performed balancing feats never seen before as they tried to keep vertical. There were cries of caution and desperate warnings ringing through Haiti's hell on earth as the work proceeded valiantly in the shattered capital of Port au Prince. Volunteers had to wear masks or bandanas over their faces to work in the ubiquitous stink of rotting corpses. Many were seen vomiting and coughing. The dust that carried the stench also half choked them.

Ambulances, sirens screaming, ran futile missions, crazily jumping up and down as they negotiated one pile of loose rubble after another, always in danger of capsizing. Survivors anxious to secure their help for severely wounded loved ones ran alongside screaming profanities and beating the sides of the ambulances until they were left in the wake of the racing vehicles. Some noticed the incongruous sight of a lonely cyclist, above all things strangely swaying about the place while trying to keep his balance, all the while crying to the world, "Water. Please, give me water. My child is dying!"

The second day after the carnage, at the cemetery, facing the graves, a dais had been erected with what passed for an altar of sorts. Grieving parishioners brought their ravaged souls, broken bodies, and tears, dressed in flowers and crosses. The diminutive and almost emaciated figure of the presiding priest, a Father Henri Rousseau, came to the steps, which he climbed with difficulty. He stood silently. Not seconds but many minutes passed, and those who came for solace and explanation asked why they had been so sorely punished. They were looking for answers. Father Rousseau knew that, and he had none to offer. His lean body quivered. He was dishevelled, all the worse for wear, and naturally looked exhausted. All the while, tremors ran through the assembly; the timid amongst them would cry out and cling desperately to anyone nearest to them, but no one left.

His hands extended, palms upturned, his gaze moved from left to right, and still the silence ran into their mystery. The silence was the silence of the dead. It lasted a long time. It seemed forever. Faces looked painfully and angrily at the lonely and hurting figure of the priest. The mystery grew, palpable and unnerving. Then his voice spilt out with some effort. It was at first cracked and little more than a stutter, afflicted with a sort of guilt at what he planned to say. The hands that he held out to his flock trembled.

"You have heard it said from the altar of what was our cathedral, you have heard it said from the days you were first able to speak and understand that our God is a God of love and justice, our defender and source of comfort and strength."

He stopped. His hand cupped his face, and he gazed out at all who stood there before him. His eyes blazing, he clenched his right fist and punched the air. "The Old Testament has its Yahweh. It's God of death. For us today, the God of death is the death of God. This God is powerless and reflects our own powerlessness. You cannot lift your hands to God for help; use them instead for burying your dead and rebuilding the cathedral, where a new faith must be born. Go to your homes and start to rebuild them for your families. Go to the broken homes of your neighbours and rebuild the community. Today we must search for new answers. Asia has its Killing Fields of Cambodia. Europe has its Holocaust. In the Americas, we today have our Haiti, our Port-au-Prince. In your spiritual journey, you are at a crossroads and have a choice to make. It must be made without anger. When we bury our dead, let us bury that anger. The new road, if there is to be a new road, must not be polluted with anger. Let your pain bless the way ahead. It is where you must turn. We will need new directions, a new vision, a new heaven, and a new God."

His eyes blazed with an evolutionary ardour. His pain could not be contained. His clerical discipline was fully compromised. His parishioners stared with disbelief at his ranting. Some of the bolder ones nodded their support, tentatively and almost fearfully but with fateful acceptance. Truth sometimes can be aborted; sometimes it has a dangerous birth. The consequence of the earthquake had an earth-shaking consequence at Port-au-Prince that day. Even as Father Rousseau spoke, the quakes shifted the earth around them all, and behind him masonry from the great cathedral kept falling off with an ongoing rumble, but soon no one was looking around with alarm. Fear seemed to have been excised from their stupefied lives, which were now too numbed with grief.

Long afterwards, the aftershocks seemed to have a life of their own. The earth still shook slightly, the tremors not too eager to leave. The tremors on earth ran tremors in a distant heaven. The light that poured out of the parted clouds was the light from a new heaven.